**She tried to pull away, but his hold was firm. "I'm not your prisoner. You're not responsible for me."**

He was close enough that she could see the muscle in his jaw jerk. "I am. Make no mistake about that."

His bare chest loomed close enough that all she had to do was reach out and she would be touching his naked skin. She let her eyes drift down across his chest, following the line of hair as it tapered down into the open V of his unbuttoned jeans.

She flicked her eyes up. His breath was shallow, drawn through just slightly open lips. His eyes seemed even darker.

And then he closed the distance between them and pulled her body up next to his, fitting her curves into his strength.

# BEVERLY LONG

## FOR THE BABY'S SAKE

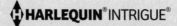

For Mary, Linda, Karen and David. Family,
and friends, too. We're lucky!

Recycling programs
for this product may
not exist in your area.

ISBN-13: 978-0-373-69703-8

FOR THE BABY'S SAKE

Copyright © 2013 by Beverly R. Long

Printed in U.S.A.

www.Harlequin.com

# ABOUT THE AUTHOR

As a child, Beverly Long used to take a flashlight to bed so that she could hide under the covers and read. Once a teenager, more often than not, the books she chose were romance novels. Now she gets to keep the light on as long as she wants, and there's always a romance novel on her nightstand. With both a bachelor's and a master's degree in business and more than twenty years of experience as a human resources director, she now enjoys the opportunity to write her own stories. She considers her books to be a great success if they compel the reader to stay up way past their bedtime.

Beverly loves to hear from readers. Visit www.beverlylong.com or like her at www.facebook.com/BeverlyLong.Romance.

## Books by Beverly Long

# CAST OF CHARACTERS

*Liz Mayfield*—Her dedication to helping pregnant teens is admirable, but is she too trusting of Mary Thorton?

*Sawyer Montgomery*—He's been chasing Dantel Mirandez for over a year and now all he needs is Mary Thorton's testimony to put the man behind bars.

*Mary Thorton*—She's a pregnant teenager who may be the only eyewitness to a brutal slaying. But is she really just an innocent bystander?

*Dantel Mirandez*—He runs a big illegal drug operation, but he may have made a mistake that will finally send him to prison.

*Jamison Curtiss*—He's the executive director of Options for Caring Mothers (OCM). He'd do most anything to save his small business.

*Howard Fraypish*—He's been OCM's attorney for years, and he's Jamison's best friend, too.

*Grandma Marvis*—Does she really care about Mary or does she know something about her disappearance that she's not saying?

# Chapter One

Liz Mayfield had kicked off her shoes long before lunch, and now, with her bare feet tucked under her butt, she simply ignored the sweat that trickled down her spine. It had to be ninety in the shade. At least ninety-five in her small, lower-level office.

It was the kind of day for pool parties and frosty drinks in pretty glasses. Not the kind of day for sorting through mail and dealing with confused teenagers.

But she'd traded one in for the other years ago when she'd left her six-figure income and five weeks of vacation to take the job at Options for Caring Mothers—OCM.

It had been three years, and there were still people scratching their heads over her choice.

She picked the top envelope off the stack on the corner of her desk. Her name was scrawled across the plain white front in blue ink. The sender had spelled her last name wrong, mixing up the order of the *i* and the *e*. She slid her thumb under the flap, pulled out the single sheet of lined notebook paper and read.

And her head started to buzz.

You stupid BITCH. You going to be very sorry if you don't stop messing in stuff thats not your busines.

The egg-salad sandwich she'd had for lunch rumbled in her stomach. Still holding the notebook paper with one hand, she cupped her other hand over her mouth. She swallowed hard twice, and once she thought she might have it under control, she unfolded her legs and stretched them far enough that she could slip both feet into her sandals. And for some crazy reason, she felt better once she had shoes on, as if she was more prepared.

She braced the heels of her hands against the edge of her scratched metal desk and pushed. Her old chair squeaked as it rolled two feet and then came to a jarring stop when a wheel jammed against a big crack in the tile floor.

Who would have sent her something like that? What did they mean that she was going to be *very sorry?* And when the heck was her heart going to stop pounding?

She stood and walked around her desk, making a very deliberate circle. On her third trip around, she worked up enough nerve to look more closely at the envelope. It had a stamp and a postmark from three days earlier but no return address. With just the nail on her pinkie finger, she flipped the envelope over. There was nothing on the back.

Her mail had been gathering dust for days. She'd had a packed schedule, and it probably would have sat another day if her one o'clock hadn't canceled. That made her feel marginally better. If nothing had happened yet to make her *very sorry,* it was probably just some idiot trying to freak her out.

That, however, didn't stop her from dropping to the floor like a sack of potatoes when she heard a noise outside her small window. On her hands and knees, she peered around the edge of her desk and felt like a fool when she looked through the open ground-level window and saw it was only Mary Thorton arriving for her two-o'clock appointment. She could see the girl's thin white legs with the terribly annoying skull tattoo just above her right knee.

Liz got up and brushed her dusty hands off on her denim shorts. The door opened and Mary, her ponytail, freckles and still-thin arms all strangely at odds with her round stomach, walked in. She picked up an OCM brochure that Liz kept on a rack by the door and started fanning herself. "I am never working in a basement when I get older," she said.

"I hope you don't have to," Liz said, grateful that her voice sounded normal. She sat in her chair and pulled it up to the desk. Using her pinkie again, she flipped the notebook paper over so that the blank side faced up.

Mary had already taken a seat on one of the two chairs in front of the desk. Pieces of strawberry blond hair clung to her neck, and her mascara was smudged around her pale blue eyes. She slouched in the chair, with her arms resting on her stomach.

"How do you feel?" Liz asked. The girl looked tired.

"Fat. And I'm sweating like a pig," Mary replied.

Liz, careful not to touch or look at the notebook paper, reached for the open manila folder that she'd pulled from her drawer earlier that morning. She scanned her notes from Mary's last visit. "How's your job at the drugstore?"

"I quit."

Mary had taken the job less than three weeks earlier. It had been the last in a string of jobs since becoming Liz's client four months ago. Most had lasted only a few days or a week at best at the others. The bosses were stupid, the hours were too many or too few, the location too far. The list went on and on—countless reasons not to keep a job.

"Why, Mary?"

She shrugged her narrow shoulders. "I gave a few friends a little discount on their makeup. Stupid boss made a big deal out of it."

"Imagine that. Now what do you plan to do?"

"I've been thinking about killing myself."

It was the one thing Mary could have said that made Liz grasp for words. "How would you do it, Mary?" she asked, sounding calmer than she felt.

"I don't know. Nothing bloody. Maybe pills. Or I might just walk off the end of Navy Pier. They say drowning is pretty peaceful."

No plan. That was good. Was it just shock talk, something destined to get Mary the attention that she seemed to crave?

"Sometimes it seems like the only answer," Mary said. She stared at her round stomach. "You know what I mean?"

Liz did know, better than most. She leaned back in her chair and looked up at the open street-level window. Three years ago, it had been a day not all that different from today. Maybe not as hot but there'd been a similar stillness in the air.

There'd been no breeze to carry the scent of death. Nothing that had prepared her for walking into that house and seeing sweet Jenny, with the deadly razor blade just inches from her limp hand, lying in the red pool of death.

Yeah, Liz knew. She just wished she didn't.

"No one would probably even notice," Mary said, her lower lip trembling.

Liz got up, walked around the desk and sat in the chair next to the teen. The vinyl covering on the seat, cracked in places, scratched her bare legs. She clasped Mary's hand and held it tight. "I would notice."

With her free hand, Mary played with the hem of her maternity shorts. "Some days," she said, "I want this baby so much, and there are other days that I can't stand it. It's like this weird little bug has gotten into my stomach, and it keeps growing and growing until it's going to explode, and there will be bug pieces everywhere."

Liz rubbed her thumb across the top of Mary's hand.

"Mary, it's okay. You're very close to your due date. It's natural to be scared."

"I'm not scared."

*Of course not.* "Have you thought any more about whether you intend to keep the baby or give it up for adoption?"

"It's not a baby. It's a bug. You got some bug parents lined up?" Mary rolled her eyes.

"I can speak with our attorney," Liz said, determined to stay on topic. "Mr. Fraypish has an excellent record of locating wonderful parents."

Mary stared at Liz, her eyes wide open. She didn't look happy or sad. Interested or bored. Just empty.

Liz stood up and stretched, determined that Mary wouldn't see her frustration. The teen had danced around the adoption issue for months, sometimes embracing it and other times flatly rejecting it. But she needed to make a decision. Soon.

Liz debated whether she should push. Mary continued to stare, her eyes focused somewhere around Liz's chin. Neither of them said a word.

Outside her window, a car stopped with a sudden squeal of brakes. Liz looked up just as the first bullet hit the far wall.

Noise thundered as more bullets spewed through the open window, sending chunks of plaster flying. Liz grabbed for Mary, pulling the pregnant girl to the floor. She covered the teen's body with her own, doing her best to keep her weight off the girl's stomach.

It stopped as suddenly as it had started. She heard the car speed off, the noise fading fast.

Liz jerked away from Mary. "Are you okay?"

The teen stared at her stomach. "I think so," she said.

Liz could see the girl reach for her familiar indifference, but it had been too quick, too frightening, too close. Tears welled up in the teen's eyes, and they rolled down her smooth, freckled cheeks. With both hands, she hugged her middle. "I didn't mean it. I don't want to die. I don't want my baby to die."

Liz had seen Mary angry, defensive, even openly hostile. But she'd never seen her cry. "I know, sweetie. I know." She reached to hug her but stopped when she heard the front door of OCM slam open and the thunder of footsteps on the wooden stairs.

Her heart rate sped up, and she hurriedly got to her feet, moving in front of Mary. The closed office door swung open. She saw the gun, and for a crazy minute, she thought the man holding it had come back to finish what he'd started. She'd been an idiot not to take the threat seriously. Some kind of strange noise squeaked out of her throat.

"It's all right," the man said. "I'm Detective Sawyer Montgomery with Chicago Police, ma'am. Are either of you hurt?"

It took her a second or two to process that this man wasn't going to hurt her. Once it registered, it seemed as if her bones turned to dust, and she could barely keep her body upright. He must have sensed that she was just about to go down for the count because he shoved his gun back into his shoulder holster and grabbed her waist to steady her.

"Take a breath," he said. "Nice and easy."

She closed her eyes and focused on sucking air in through her nose and blowing it out her mouth. All she could think about was that he didn't sound like a Chicago cop. He sounded Southern, like the cool, sweet tea she'd enjoyed on hot summer evenings a lifetime ago. Smooth.

After four or five breaths, she opened her eyes. He looked at her, saw that she was back among the living and let go of her waist. He backed up a step. "Are you hurt?" he repeated.

"We're okay," she said, focusing on him. He wore gray dress pants, a wrinkled white shirt and a red tie that was loose at the collar. He had a police radio clipped to his belt, and though it was turned low, she could hear the background noise of Chicago's finest at work.

He reached into his shirt pocket, pulled out a badge, flipped it open and held it steady, giving her a chance to read.

"Thank you, Detective Montgomery," she said.

He nodded and pivoted to show it to Mary. Once she nodded, he flipped it shut and returned it to his pocket. Then he extended a hand to help Mary up off the floor.

Mary hesitated, then took it. Once up, she moved several feet away. Detective Montgomery didn't react. Instead he pulled his radio from his belt. "Squad, this is 5162. I'm inside at 229 Logan Street. No injuries to report. Backup is still requested to secure the exterior."

Liz stared at the cop. He had the darkest brown eyes—almost, but not quite, black. His hair was brown and thick and looked as if it had recently been trimmed. His skin was tanned, and his lips had a very nice shape.

Best-looking cop she'd seen in some time.

In fact, only cop she'd seen in some time. Logan Street wasn't in a great neighborhood but was quiet in comparison to the streets that ran a couple blocks to the south. As such, it didn't get much attention from the police.

And yet, Detective Montgomery had been inside OCM less than a minute after the shooting. That didn't make sense. She stepped forward, putting herself between the detective and Mary.

"How did you get here so quickly?" she asked.

He hesitated for just a second. "I was parked outside."

"That was coincidental," she said. "I'm not generally big on coincidences."

He shrugged and pulled a notebook out of his pocket. "May I have your name, please?"

His look and his attitude were all business. His voice was pure pleasure. The difference in the two caught her off balance, making her almost forgive that he was being deliberately evasive. There was a reason he'd been parked outside, but he wasn't ready to cough it up. She was going to have to play the game his way.

"Liz Mayfield," she said. "I'm one of three counselors here at OCM. Options for Caring Mothers," she added. "This is Mary Thorton."

The introduction wasn't necessary. The girl had been keeping him up at nights. Sawyer knew her name, her social security number, her address. Hell, he knew her favorite breakfast cereal. Three empty boxes of Fruit Loops in her garbage had been pretty hard to miss. "Miss Thorton," he said, nodding at the teen before turning back to the counselor. "Is there anybody else in the building?"

The woman shook her head. "Carmen was here earlier, but she left to take her brother to the orthodontist. Cynthia, she's the third counselor, just works in the mornings. We have a part-time receptionist, too, but she's not here today. Oh, and Jamison is getting ready for a fund-raiser. He's working off-site."

"Who's Jamison?"

"He's the boss."

"Okay. Why don't the two of you—"

Sawyer stopped when he heard his partner let loose their call numbers. He turned the volume up on his radio.

"Squad, this is 5162, following a gray Lexus, license Adam, John, David, 7, 4, 9. I lost him, somewhere around Halsted and 35th. Repeat, lost him. Keep an eye out, guys."

Sawyer wasn't surprised. He and Robert had been parked a block down the street. Sawyer had jumped out, and Robert had given chase, but the shooter had at least a two-block advantage. In a crowded city, filled with alleys and side streets, that was a lot. Every cop on the street in that general vicinity would be on the watch now, but Sawyer doubted it would do any good. Mirandez's boys would have dumped the car by now. He turned the volume on his radio back down.

"Why don't you two have a seat?" he said, trying hard to maintain a hold on his emotions. They hadn't gotten the shooter, but maybe—just maybe—he had Mary Thorton in a position where she'd want to talk.

The counselor sat. Mary continued to stand until Liz Mayfield patted the chair next to her.

Facing both women, he said, "I'd like to ask you a few questions. Are you feeling up to that?"

"You okay?" Liz Mayfield asked Mary.

The girl shrugged. "I suppose."

The woman nodded at Sawyer. "Shoot," she said.

Mary snorted, and the pretty counselor's cheeks turned pink. "Sorry," she mumbled. "We're ready. Proceed. Begin."

Wow. She was a Beach Boys song—a regular California girl—with her smooth skin and thick, blond hair that hung down to the middle of her back. She wore a sleeveless white cotton shirt and denim shorts, and her toenails were the brightest pink he'd ever seen.

What the hell was she doing in a basement on the south side of Chicago?

He knew what he was doing there. He was two minutes and two hundred yards behind Dantel Mirandez. Like he had been for the past eighteen months.

And the son of a bitch had slipped away again.

Sawyer crossed his legs at the ankles and leaned back against the desk, resting his butt on the corner. He focused his attention on the teenager. She sat slouched in her chair, staring at the floor. "Ms. Thorton, any ideas about who is responsible for this shooting?"

Out of the corner of his eye, he saw Liz Mayfield sit up straighter in her chair. "I—"

He held up his hand, stopping her. "If you don't mind, I'd like to give Ms. Thorton a chance to answer first."

"I don't know anything, Cop," the teen said, her voice hard with irritation.

Damn. "You're sure?"

Mary raised her chin. "Yeah. What kind of cop are you? Haven't you heard about people in cars with guns? They shoot things. Duh. That's why they call them drive-by shooters."

It looked as if she planned to stick to the same old story. He walked over to the window and looked out. Two squad cars had arrived. He knew the officers would systematically work their way through the crowd that had gathered, trying to find out if anybody had seen anything that would be helpful. He didn't hold out much hope. In this neighborhood, even if somebody saw something, they wouldn't be that likely to talk. He heard a noise behind him and turned.

"I'm out of here." Mary pushed on the arms of her chair and started to get up. "I've got things to do."

He wasn't letting her off the hook that easy. "Sit down," he instructed. "We're not done."

"You can't tell me what to do," Mary shouted.

*You can't tell me what to do.* The words bounced off the walls, sharp, quick blows, taking Sawyer back seventeen years. Just a kid himself, he'd alternated between begging, demanding, bribing, whatever he'd thought would work. But that angry teenage girl hadn't listened to him, either. She'd continued to pump heroin into her veins, and his son, his precious infant son, had paid the ultimate price.

Sawyer bit the inside of his lip. "Sit," he said.

Liz Mayfield stood. "Detective, may I talk to you privately?"

He gave her a quick glance. "In a minute." He turned his

attention back to Mary. "I'm going to ask you one more time. What do you know about this shooting?"

"What I know is that you talk funny."

He heard Liz Mayfield's quick intake of breath, but the woman remained silent.

"Is that right?" Sawyer rubbed his chin, debating how much he should share. "Maybe I do. Where I come from, everybody talks like this. Where I come from, two drive-by shootings in one week is something worthy of note."

Mary lowered her chin. Liz Mayfield, who had remained standing, cocked her head to the side and studied Mary. "Two?" she asked.

Sawyer didn't wait for Mary. "While Ms. Thorton shopped in a convenience store just three days ago, the front windows got shot out," he said.

"Mary?"

Was it surprise or hurt that he heard in the counselor's voice?

The teen didn't answer. The silence stretched for another full minute before Liz tried again. "What's going on here?" she asked.

"There ain't nothing going on here," Mary said. "Besides me getting bored out of my mind, that is."

"Somebody's going to get killed one of these days." Sawyer paced in front of the two women, stopping in front of Mary. "How would you like it if Ms. Mayfield had gotten a bullet in the back of her head?"

"I got rights," Mary yelled.

"Be quiet," he said. "Use some of that energy and tell me about Mirandez."

"Who?" the counselor asked.

Sawyer didn't respond, his attention focused on Mary. He saw her hand grip the wooden arm of the chair.

"Well?" Sawyer prompted. "Are you going to pretend you don't know who I'm talking about?"

"Stupid cops," Mary said, shaking her head.

He'd been called worse. Twice already today. "Come on, Mary," he said. "Before somebody dies."

Mary leaned close to her counselor. "I don't know what he's talking about. Honest, I don't. You've got to believe me." A tear slid down the girl's pale face, dripping onto her round stomach. He looked away. He didn't want to think about her baby.

"If I can go home now," Mary said, looking up at Liz Mayfield, "I'll come back tomorrow. We can talk about the adoption."

The woman stared at the teen for a long minute before turning to him. "Mary says she doesn't know anything about the shooting. I'm not sure what else we can tell you."

Sawyer settled back against the desk and contemplated his next words. "That's it? That's all either of you has to say?"

Liz Mayfield shrugged. "I'd still like a minute of your time," she said, "but if you don't have any other questions for Mary, can she go home?" She brushed her hair back from her face. "It has been a rather unpleasant day."

Maybe he needed to describe in graphic detail exactly what unpleasant looked like.

"Please," she said.

She looked tired and pale, and he remembered that she'd already about passed out once. "Fine," he said. "She can go."

Liz Mayfield extended her hand to Mary, helping the girl out of the chair. She wrapped her arm around Mary's freckled shoulder, and they left the room.

He had his back toward the door, his face turned toward the open window, scanning the street, when she came back. "I'm just curious," he said without turning around. "You saw her when I said his name. She knows something. You know it, and I know it. How come you let her walk away?"

"Who's Mirandez?" she asked.

He turned around. He wanted to see her face. "Dantel Mirandez is scum. The worst kind of scum. He's the guy who makes it possible for third graders to buy a joint at recess. And for their older brothers and sisters to be heroin addicts by the time they're twelve. And for their parents to spend their grocery money on—"

"I think I get it, Detective."

"Yeah, well, get this. Mirandez isn't just your neighborhood dealer. He runs a big operation. Maybe as much as ten percent of all the illegal drug traffic in Chicago. Millions of dollars pass through his organization. He employs hundreds. Not bad for a twenty-six-year-old punk."

"How do you know Mary is involved with him?"

"It's my job to know. She's been his main squeeze for the past six months—at least."

"It doesn't make sense. Why would he try to hurt her?"

"We don't think he's trying to hurt her. It's more like he's trying to get her attention, to make sure she remembers that he's the boss. To make sure that she remembers that he can get to her at any time, at any place."

"I don't understand."

"Three weeks ago, during one of his transactions, he killed a man. Little doubt that it wasn't the first time. But word on the street is that this time, your little Miss Mary was with him. She saw it."

"Oh, my God. I had no idea."

She looked as if she might faint again. He pushed a chair in her direction. She didn't even look at it. He watched her, relaxing when a bit of color returned to her face.

"I'm sure you didn't," he said. "The tip came in about a week ago that Mary saw the hit. And then the convenience store got shot up. She got questioned at the scene, but she didn't offer anything up about Mirandez. I've been following her ever since. It wasn't a coincidence that my partner and I were parked a block away. We saw a car come around the corner, slow down. Before we could do anything, they had a gun stuck out the window, blowing this place up. We called it in, and I jumped out to come inside. My partner went after them. As you may have heard," he said, motioning to his radio, "they got away."

"It sounded like you got a license plate."

"Not that it will do us any good. It's a pretty safe bet that the car was hot. Stolen," he added.

"Do you know for sure that it was Mirandez who shot out my window? Did you actually see him?"

"I'm sure it wasn't him pulling the trigger. He rarely does his own dirty work. It was likely someone further down the food chain."

She swallowed hard. "You may be right, Detective. And I'm willing to try to talk to Mary, to try to convince her to cooperate with the police. You have to understand that my first priority is her. She doesn't have anyone else."

"She has Mirandez."

"She's never said a word about him."

"I assume he's the father of the baby," he said. "That fact is probably the only thing that's keeping her alive right now. Otherwise, I think she'd be expendable. Everybody is to this guy."

Liz shook her head. "He's not the father of her baby."

"How do you know?"

She hesitated. "Because I've met the father. He's a business major at Loyola."

"That doesn't make sense. Why isn't he tending to his own business? What kind of man lets his girlfriend and his unborn child get mixed up with people like Mirandez? He knows about the baby?"

"Yes. But he's not interested."

"He said that?"

"Mary is considering adoption. When the paternity of a baby is known, we require the father's consent as well as the mother's."

"I guess they're not teaching responsibility in college anymore." Sawyer flexed his hand, wishing he had about three minutes with college boy.

"Can't download it," she answered.

Sawyer laughed, his anger dissipating a bit. "And where does Mirandez fit into this?" he asked. "You saw her face when I said his name. She knows him all right. The question is, what else does she know?"

"It's hard to say. She's not an easy person to read."

"How old is she?"

"She turned eighteen last month. Legally an adult but still very young, if you know what I mean."

"Yeah, well, she's gonna be young, foolish and dead if she doesn't get away from Mirandez. It's only a matter of time." He wanted Liz to understand the severity. "Otherwise, if I can prove she was at that murder scene, then she's an accessory and that baby is gonna be born in jail."

"Well, that's clear enough." She turned her head to look at her desk. She took a deep breath. "It may not have anything to do with Mary."

He lowered his chin and studied her. "Why do you say that?"

She walked over to the desk and flipped over a piece of notebook paper. She pointed at it and then the envelope next to it. "They go together. I opened it about a half hour ago."

He looked down and read it quickly. When he jerked his

head up, she stood there, looking calmer than he felt. "Any idea who sent this?"

She shook her head. "So maybe this has nothing to do with Mary. Maybe, just maybe, you were busting her chops for nothing."

For some odd reason, her slightly sarcastic tone made him smile. "I wasn't busting her chops," he said. "That was me making polite conversation. First time you ever get something like this?"

"Yes."

"Anybody really pissed off at you?"

"I work with pregnant teenagers and when possible with the fathers, too. Most of them are irritated with me at one time or another. It's my job to make them deal with things they'd sometimes rather ignore."

He supposed it was possible that the shooting wasn't Mirandez's work, but the similarities between it and the shooting at the convenience store were too strong to be ignored. "I imagine you touched this?"

She nodded.

"Anybody else have access to your mail?"

"Our receptionist. She sorts it."

"Okay. I'll need both your prints so that we can rule them out."

She blew out a breath. "Fine. I've got her home number. By the way, they spelled my name wrong," she said. "That doesn't necessarily mean it's not someone who knows me. Given that *business* is also spelled wrong and the grammar isn't all that great, I'd say we're not dealing with a genius."

"They still got their point across."

She smiled at him, and he noticed not for the first time that Liz Mayfield was one damn fine-looking woman. "That they did," she said. "Loud and clear."

"Why don't you have a seat? I'll get an evidence tech out

here to take your prints. That will take a few minutes. In the meantime, I've got a few questions."

She rolled her eyes. "I'll just bet you do," she said before she dutifully sat down.

## Chapter Two

"Hey, Montgomery, you owe me ten bucks. I told you the Cubs would lose to St. Louis. When are you going to learn?"

Sawyer fished two fives out of his pocket. He hadn't expected his boys to win. But he'd been a fan since coming to Chicago two years earlier and going to his first Cubs game at Wrigley Field. He wasn't sentimental enough to believe it was because of the ivy growing on the walls that it somehow reminded him of home. He liked to think it was because the Cubs, no matter if they were winning or losing, were always the underdog. Sort of like cops.

He folded the bills and tossed them at his partner. "Here. Now shut up. Why does the lieutenant want to see us?"

"I don't know. I got the same page you did." Robert Hanson pulled a thick telephone book out of his desk drawer. "It's a damn shame. Veronica spent the night, and she's really at her best in the morning. Very enthusiastic."

"Which one is Veronica?"

"Blonde. Blue eyes. Nice rack."

That described most of the women Robert dated. Sawyer heard the door and looked up. Lieutenant Fischer walked in.

"Gentlemen," their boss greeted them, dropping a thick green file on the wood desk. "We've got a problem."

Robert sat up straighter in his chair. Sawyer stared at his

boss. The man looked every one of his fifty years. "What's up?" Sawyer asked.

"We've got another dead body. Looks like the guy was beat up pretty good before somebody shot him in the head."

"Mirandez?" Sawyer hissed.

"Probably. Our guys ID'd the deceased. Bobbie Morage."

Sawyer looked at Robert. "Morage was tight with Mirandez until recently."

Robert nodded. "Rumor has it that Morage was skimming off the top. Taking product home in his pockets."

Lieutenant Fischer closed his eyes and leaned his head back. "No honor among thieves or killers."

"Any witnesses?" Sawyer asked.

His boss opened his eyes. "None. Got one hysterical maid at the Rotayne Hotel. She found him on her way to the Dumpster. Look, we've got to get this guy. This makes three in the past two months. Eight in the past year."

Sawyer could do the math. He wanted Mirandez more than he'd wanted anybody in fifteen years of wearing a badge.

"Are you sure you can't get Mary Thorton to talk?" The lieutenant stood in front of Sawyer, his arms folded across his chest.

"I don't know. Like I told you yesterday, she's either in it up to her eyeballs, or she's just a dumb young kid with a smart mouth who doesn't know anything. I'm not sure which."

"What about her counselor? What was her name?"

"Liz. Elizabeth, I guess. Last name is Mayfield."

"Can she help us?"

"I don't know." Sawyer shook his head. "If anyone can get to Mary, I think she's the one. She said she'd try."

"We need the girlfriend. Push the counselor if you need to."

Sawyer understood Lieutenant Fischer's anxiety. People

were dying. "She does have her own issues," he said, feeling the need to defend the woman.

Lieutenant Fischer rubbed a hand across his face. "I know. You get any prints off the note she got?"

"Nothing that we couldn't match up to her or the receptionist. We got a couple partials, and we're tracking down the mail carrier to rule him or her out. I don't know. It could be coincidence that she got this and then Mirandez went after Mary Thorton again."

"I don't believe in coincidence," Lieutenant Fischer said, his voice hard.

Sawyer didn't much, either. "I'll go see her now."

"I'll go with you," Robert offered, clearly resigned that Veronica was an opportunity lost.

*Blonde. Blue eyes. Nice rack.* Liz Mayfield had green eyes, but other than that, she was just Robert's type. "No," Sawyer said, not even looking at Robert.

"Hey, it's no problem. I like to watch you try to use that old-fashioned Southern charm."

"I don't need any help." Sawyer looked at his lieutenant and got the nod of approval he needed.

"Fine," Robert said. "Go ahead and drag your sorry ass over there again. I'll just stay here. In the air-conditioning."

Lieutenant Fischer shook his head. "No, you don't. You're going to the hotel to interview the maid again. She doesn't speak much English."

"Doesn't anybody else speak Spanish?" Robert moaned.

"Not like you do. I've got officers who grew up in Mexico that don't speak it as well."

Robert grinned broadly. "It's hell to be brilliant." He ducked out the door right before the telephone book hit it.

A HALF HOUR LATER, Sawyer parked his car in front of the brick two-story. He walked past a couple brown-eyed, brown-skinned children, carefully stepping around the pictures they'd created on the sidewalk with colored chalk.

Sawyer nodded at the two old men sitting on the steps. When he'd left OCM the day before, he'd taken the time to speak to them personally, hoping they'd seen the shooter. From his vehicle, just minutes before the arrival of what he still believed was Mirandez's band of dirty men, he'd seen them in the same spot, chatting.

They'd seen the shooter. It didn't help much. He'd worn a face mask.

He took the steps of OCM two at a time. He just needed to get inside, talk to Liz Mayfield and get the hell out of there. Before he did something stupid like touch her. He'd thought of her skin for most of the night. Her soft, silky skin. With legs that went on forever.

Sawyer glanced down at the street-level window. Plywood covered the opening, keeping both the sun and unwanted visitors out. He didn't stop to wonder how unwelcome he might be. He walked through the deserted hallway and down the steps. He knocked once on the closed door and then again when no one answered. He tried the knob, but it wouldn't turn.

"She left early."

Sawyer whirled around. He'd been so focused on the task that he hadn't heard the woman come up behind him.

"Sorry." She laughed at him. "Didn't mean to scare you."

Looking at her could scare almost anybody. She had bright red hair, blue eyeliner, black lips, and she wore a little bit of a skirt and shirt, showing more skin than material. She couldn't have been much older than eighteen. If she had been his daughter, he'd have locked her in the house until she found some clothes and washed the god-awful makeup off.

His son would have been just about her age. "What's your name?" he asked.

"Nicole." She held up the palm of her hand and wriggled her fingers. "Don't you recognize me?"

She was the part-time receptionist who had gotten her prints taken. An evidence tech had taken care of it for him. He'd been busy filling out case reports—one for the shooting, a separate one for Liz Mayfield's threat. "Sorry. Thanks for doing that, by the way."

"I'd do almost anything for Liz. Like I said, though, she's not here. She left early. Maybe to get ready for the dance."

Sawyer tried to concentrate. "A dance?"

"OCM is having a dance. A fund-raiser. Jamison says we're going to have to shut the doors if donations don't pick up."

Sawyer had finally had the opportunity to talk on the telephone with Jamison Curtiss, the executive director of OCM, late the evening before. The man had flitted between outrage at both the shooting and the note Liz Mayfield had received, to worry about the bad press for OCM, to despair about the neighborhood all in a matter of minutes.

Sawyer had told himself, several times while he was shaving this morning, that it had been that conversation that had spurred dreams of Liz Mayfield. Otherwise, there'd have been no reason to take his work home, to take it literally to bed with him.

Dreaming about a woman was something Robert would do.

"Dinner is two hundred bucks a plate," the girl continued. "Can you believe that? Like, I'd cook 'em dinner for half that."

"Where?"

"Like, at my house."

Sawyer shook his head. "No, where's the dinner?"

"At the Rotayne Hotel. Pretty fancy, huh?"

"As fancy as they get." *As long as they keep the dead bodies hidden in the alley.* "What time does it start?"

"Dinner's at seven. My grandmother wanted me to go. Thought I might meet a nice young man there." She wrinkled her nose.

"Not interested?" he asked.

She shook her head. "Last one I met got me knocked up. Guess Grandma kind of forgot about that. I don't know what I would have done if Liz hadn't helped me find a family for my baby. Now she's living in the suburbs. Like, with a mom and dad and two cats." The girl's eyes filled with tears.

"Uh…" He was so far out of his league here.

"Anyway," she said, sniffing loudly. She tossed her hair back. "She's the best. Some lawyer guy helps her. He talks fast, drinks too much and wears ugly ties. Easy to spot."

"What's his name?" Sawyer asked.

"Howard Fraypish. Liz went to the dance with him."

Sawyer pulled his notebook out of his suit coat pocket and made a note of the name. Yesterday, after they'd gotten Liz Mayfield's prints, he'd asked her whether she was seeing anybody. It was a legitimate question, he'd told himself at the time.

She hadn't even blinked. Said that she hadn't dated anyone for over a year.

Going to a dance with somebody sounded like a date.

"I think she just feels sorry for him," the girl added.

So, she and lawyer guy weren't close. Maybe there was someone else. He had a right to ask. Maybe the connection wasn't Mary or Mirandez. Maybe the shooter's target had been the pretty counselor. It wouldn't be the first time a spurned love interest had crossed the line. "She seeing anybody else?"

"Not that I'm aware of."

He was glad that Liz hadn't lied to him. But it still surprised him. A woman who looked like Liz Mayfield shouldn't have trouble getting a date. She had the kind of face and body that made a man stupid.

He'd made that mistake once in his life. He wouldn't make it again.

HE TRIED TO REMEMBER THAT, two hours later, when he watched her glide around the room. She had on a long, dark blue dress. It flowed from her narrow waist, falling just shy of her ankles. It puffed out when she turned.

She'd pulled her hair up, leaving just a few strands down. Sawyer rubbed his fingers together, imagining the feel of the silky texture. The dress had a high collar and sleeves ending just below the elbow. She barely showed any skin at all, and she was the sexiest woman there.

Classy. It was the only word he could think of.

Determined to get it over with, Sawyer strode across the dance floor, ignoring the startled whispers or shocked glances in his wake. He felt as out of place as he knew he looked with his faded blue jeans and his beat-up leather jacket. He'd shed his suit earlier that evening before suddenly deciding that he needed to see Liz Mayfield tonight. She'd had her twenty-four hours. It wasn't his fault that she was a party girl and wanted to dance.

He met her eyes over the shoulder of her date. Her full lips parted ever so slightly, and her face lost its color. He shrugged in return and tapped the man between them on the shoulder.

The guy, early forties and balding, turned his head slightly, frowned at Sawyer and kept dancing.

Sawyer tapped again. "I need a few minutes with Ms. Mayfield."

They stopped. When the guy made no move to let go of her, Sawyer held out his hand. She stared at it for several seconds then stepped away from her date. Suddenly she was in his arms, and they were dancing.

He wanted to say something. But his stupid mind wouldn't work. He couldn't think, couldn't talk, couldn't reason.

She smelled good—like the jasmine flowers that had grown outside his mother's kitchen window.

He wanted to pull her close and taste her. The realization hit him hard, as if someone had punched him. He wanted his tongue in her mouth, her breasts in his hands and her thighs wrapped around him. He wanted her naked under him.

Sawyer jerked back, stumbling a bit. He dropped his hands to his sides. The two of them stood still in the middle of the dance floor like two statues.

Why didn't she say something? Hell, why didn't she blink? She just kept her pretty green eyes focused on his face. Sawyer kept his breaths shallow, unwilling to let any more temptation into his lungs. "Any more letters?" he asked. He kept his voice low, not wanting others to hear.

She shook her head. "Our mail doesn't usually arrive until after lunch. I left before it got there."

"So, no news is good news?"

"For tonight."

He understood avoidance. At one point in his life, he'd perfected it. He felt silly standing in the middle of the floor. He stepped closer to Liz Mayfield, and she slipped back into his arms as if it was the most natural thing in the world.

Which didn't make sense at all because it had to have been ten years since he'd danced with a woman. It felt good. She felt good.

He really needed to remember that he wasn't here to dance. "What did your little friend have to say?" he asked.

Her body jerked, and he realized he'd been more stern than necessary. "I'm sorry," he said.

"That's fine," she said. "It's just that I...I didn't see Mary today."

"She didn't show, did she?"

Liz shook her head and jumped in with both feet. "I had to cancel most of my appointments. I didn't feel well." That much at least was true. She'd been sick after hearing Mary's voice mail. *I'm not coming today. I'll see you tomorrow at the regular time.*

Liz had tried to call her a dozen times before giving up. Dreading that Detective Montgomery would find her before she had the chance to locate Mary, she'd left the office. She'd worried that a frustrated Detective Montgomery might take matters in his own hands and track Mary down.

Liz had never expected he'd show up at the fund-raiser. But she should have known better. Detective Montgomery didn't seem like the kind of guy who gave up easily. In fact, he seemed downright tenacious. Like a dog after a bone.

She tried to hold that against him. But couldn't. While it made for an uncomfortable evening, she couldn't help appreciating the fact that he'd held her to her twenty-four hours. He took his work seriously. She could relate to that.

"Are you okay now?" he asked, sounding concerned.

She nodded, not willing to verbalize any more half-truths. From across the room, she caught Carmen's eye. She was standing behind the punch table, pouring cups for thirsty dancers. Liz could read the concern on her pretty face. She'd had that same look since Liz had told her about the letter.

Liz shook her head slightly, reassuring her. Carmen was little, but she could be a spitfire. If she thought Liz needed help, she'd come running.

"Who's that?" Detective Montgomery asked.

"Carmen Jimenez. She's a counselor, too. I think I mentioned her yesterday."

"I remember. Did you tell her about your letter?"

"Yes."

"She hasn't gotten anything similar?"

Liz shook her head.

"I've got some bad news," Detective Montgomery said. "We found another dead body this morning. Right outside of this very hotel. He'd been shot. Up until a few weeks ago, he'd been a cook for Mirandez."

"Mirandez has a cook?"

He leaned his mouth closer to her ear, and she felt the shiver run down the length of her spine. "Not like Oprah has a cook. A cook is the guy who boils down the cocaine into crack."

"Oh. My."

"People keep dying," he said. "It's my job to make it stop. If Mary knows something, it's her job to help me."

She'd been wrong. He wasn't like a dog after a bone. He wanted fresh meat. She pulled away from him, forcing the dancing to stop. She couldn't think when he had his arms around her, let alone when his mouth was that close. "If you had enough to arrest her," she protested, "you'd have done it yesterday. You don't have anything but a wild guess."

He had more than that. The tip had come from one of their own. It had taken Fluentes two years to work his way inside. Sawyer didn't intend to sacrifice him now.

*Push the counselor.* He could hear Lieutenant Fischer's words almost as clearly as if the man stood behind him. "She was there. And you need to convince her to tell us what she saw. She needs to tell us everything. Then we'll protect her."

"You'll protect her?"

"Yeah." For some reason Liz's disbelieving tone set Sawyer's teeth on edge. "That's what we do. We're cops."

"She's eight months pregnant."

"I'm aware of that. We would arrange for both her and her baby to have the medical care that they need."

"And then what?" she asked, her tone demanding.

Sawyer threw up his hands. "I don't know. I guess the baby grows up, and in twenty years, Mary's a grandmother." Sawyer rubbed the bridge of his nose. His head pounded, and the damn drums weren't helping. "Look, can we go outside?" he mumbled.

She seemed to hesitate. Sawyer let out a breath when she nodded and took off, weaving in and out of the dancers, not stopping until she reached the exit. They walked outside the hotel, and he led her far enough away that the doorman couldn't hear the conversation.

She spoke before he had the chance to question her. "I'll talk to her. She's supposed to come to OCM at eight tomorrow morning. It's her regular appointment."

"And you'll convince her to talk to us?"

"I'll talk—"

"Liz, Liz. Back here. What are you doing outside?"

Sawyer turned back toward the hotel door. Her date stood next to the doorman, wildly waving his arm. The man started walking toward them, his long legs eating up the distance.

"He doesn't know about my letter," Liz said, her voice almost a whisper. "I'd like to keep it that way."

When the man reached Liz's side, he wrapped a skinny arm around her and tugged her toward his body. For some crazy reason, Sawyer wanted to break the man's arm. In two, maybe three, places. Then maybe a kneecap next.

"You had me worried when I couldn't find you," he said.

She stepped out of the man's grasp. "Detective Montgomery is the detective assigned to the shooting at OCM." She turned back to Sawyer. "Detective Montgomery, Howard Fraypish," she said, finishing the introduction.

The guy stuck his arm out, and Sawyer returned the shake. "I'm OCM's attorney," Fraypish said.

The man's hot-pink bow tie matched his cummerbund.

"I better get going," Sawyer said. "Thanks for the information, Ms. Mayfield."

"I certainly hope you arrest the men responsible for the attack at OCM," Fraypish said. "Where were the city's finest when this happened? At the local doughnut shop?"

Was that the best the guy could do? "I don't like doughnuts," Sawyer said.

"Are you sure you're a cop?"

Liz Mayfield frowned at her date. The idiot held up both hands in mock surrender. "Just a little joke. I thought we could use some humor."

Sawyer thought a quick left followed by a sharp right would be kind of funny.

"I should have called you, Detective. Then you wouldn't have had to make a trip here," she apologized.

"Forget it." His only regret was the blue dress. He knew how good she looked in it. He wondered how long before he stopped thinking about how good she'd look without it.

LIZ WOKE UP at four in the morning. Her body needed rest, but her mind refused to cooperate. She'd left the hotel shortly after midnight. She'd been in her apartment and in bed less than ten minutes later. She'd dreamed about Mary. Sweet Mary and her baby. Sweet Mary and the faceless Dantel Mirandez. Jenny had been there, too. With her crooked smile, her flyaway blond hair blowing around her as she threw a handful of pennies into the fountain at Grant Park. Just the way she'd been the last day Liz had seen her alive. Then out of nowhere, there'd been more letters, more threats. So many that when she'd fallen down and they'd piled on top of her, they'd covered her. And she hadn't been able to breathe.

Waking up had been a relief.

She showered, put on white capri pants and a blue shirt

and caught the five-o'clock bus. Thirty minutes later, it dropped her off a block from OCM. The morning air was heavy with humidity. It had the makings of another ninety-degree day.

She entered the security code, unlocked the front door, entered and then reset the code. She didn't bother to go downstairs to her office, heading instead to the small kitchen at the rear of the first floor. She started a pot of coffee, pouring a cup before the pot was even half-full. She took a sip, burned her tongue and swallowed anyway. She needed caffeine.

While she waited for her bagel to toast, she thought about Detective Montgomery. When he'd walked away, in the wake of Howard's insults, she'd wanted to run after him, to apologize, to make him understand that she'd do what she could to help him.

As long as it didn't put Mary in any danger.

But she hadn't. When Howard had hustled her back inside the hotel, she'd gone without protest. Jamison had made it abundantly clear. Attendees had coughed up two hundred bucks a plate. If they wanted to dance, you danced. If they needed a drink, you fetched it. If they wanted conversation, you talked.

Liz had danced, fetched, talked and smiled through it all. Even after her toes had been stepped on for the eighteenth time. No politician could have done better. She'd done it on autopilot. It hadn't helped when Carmen had come up, fanning herself, and said, "Who was that?"

"Detective Montgomery," Liz had explained.

"I suspect I don't have to state the obvious," Carmen had said, "but the man is hot."

Liz had almost laughed. Carmen hadn't even heard the man talk. Or felt the man's chest muscles when he'd held her close—not too close but close enough. She hadn't smelled his clean, fresh scent.

Detective Montgomery wasn't just hot; he was *smoking* hot.

Her bagel popped just as she heard the front door open. She relaxed when she didn't hear the alarm. Who else, she wondered, was crazy enough to come to work at five-thirty in the morning?

When she heard Jamison's office door open, she almost dropped her bagel. He probably hadn't gotten home much before two.

She spread cream cheese evenly on both sides and started a second pot of coffee. Jamison was perhaps the only person on earth who loved coffee more than she did. She had her cup and her bagel balanced in one hand and had just slung her purse over her shoulder when she heard the front door close again.

She eased the kitchen door open and glanced down the narrow hallway. Empty. All the office doors remained closed. "Hello?"

No answer. She walked down the hallway, knocked on Jamison's door and then tried the handle. It didn't turn.

She walked down the steps to the lower level. Her office door and all the others were shut. "Good morning?" she sang out, a bit louder this time.

The only sound she heard was her own breathing.

Liz ran up the stairs, swearing softly when the hot coffee splashed out of the cup and burned her hand. She checked the front door. Locked. Alarm set.

She relaxed. It had to have been Jamison. What would have possessed him to come in so early and leave so quickly? She hoped nothing was wrong. She walked back downstairs and unlocked her office. It was darker than usual because no light spilled through the boarded-up window.

She had to admit that the wood made her feel better.

Maybe she'd ask Jamison to leave it that way for a while. At least until she got her nerves under control.

Rationally, she didn't put much stock in the letter. It wasn't out of the realm of possibility that one of her clients or their partners had decided to jerk her chain a little. It didn't make her feel any better, however, to think that the shooter had been aiming for Mary.

She intended to somehow make the girl open up to her, to tell her if there was any connection between her and Dantel Mirandez. But in the meantime, she needed to get busy. She sat down behind her desk and opened the top file. Mary was not the only client who was close to delivery. Just two days before, Melissa Stroud had been in Liz's office. They'd reviewed the information on Mike and Mindy Partridge, and Melissa had agreed to let the couple adopt her soon-to-be-born child. Liz needed to get the necessary information to Howard so that he could get the paperwork done.

At twenty minutes to eight, she heard the front door open again. Heavy footsteps pounded down the stairs, and within seconds, her boss stuck his head through the open doorway.

"Hey, Liz. Nice window."

She shook her head. "Morning, Jamison. How are you?"

"Exhausted. It ended up being a late night. We didn't leave the hotel until they pushed us out the door. Then Reneé and I and a couple others went out for breakfast. I didn't want to say no to any potential donors. I've got a heck of a headache, though. It was probably that last vodka tonic."

"Jamison, you know better." Liz smiled at her boss. "Had you been to bed yet when you stopped by here this morning?"

"This morning? What are you talking about?"

"You stopped in about six. I had coffee made, but you left before I could catch you."

"Liz, how many glasses of wine did you have last night?"

Liz dismissed his concern with a wave of her hand. "Two. That's my limit."

"Well, you may want to cut back to one. Reneé had set the alarm for seven, and we slept through that. I barely had time for a two-minute shower just to get here by now."

Liz shook her head, trying to make sense out of what Jamison said. "I heard the door. The alarm didn't go off. I'm sure I heard your office door open. But when I came out, there was nobody around."

"It must have been a car door."

"No, it wasn't," Liz protested.

"Then it was Cynthia or Carmen or one of the other staff. Although I can't imagine why anybody would have gotten up early after last night. What were you doing here?"

"Mary Thorton is coming at eight. I wanted to get some stuff done first." No need to tell Jamison that she'd been running from her dreams. He already thought she was losing her mind.

"Have you talked to her since the shooting? Poor kid. She must be pretty shook up."

"I'm sure she was. Detective Montgomery thinks she knows more than she's letting on."

"Is that why he came to the dance last night?"

Liz was surprised. Jamison rarely noticed anything that didn't directly concern him. But then again, Detective Montgomery had a way about him that commanded attention.

"Yes."

"At least he wasn't in uniform. That wouldn't have been good for donations. How do you think the party went?" Jamison asked, sitting down on one of Liz's chairs.

"People seemed to have a good time," Liz hedged. When his eyes lit up, her guilt vanished. He could be a bit self-centered and pushy, but Liz knew he'd do almost anything for OCM. She would, too.

Even spend an evening with Howard Fraypish, who had been Jamison's college roommate. After college, Jamison had taken a job in social services and married Reneé. Howard had gone to law school, graduated at the top of his class, married his corporate job and produced billable hours. Lots of them, evidently. The man had a huge apartment with a view of Lake Michigan, and he'd opened his own law office at least five years ago.

The two men had stayed connected over the years, and when Jamison had been hired as the executive director of OCM, he'd hired Howard's firm to handle the adoptions.

"Want a warm-up?" Jamison asked, nodding at Liz's empty cup.

"Sure."

They walked upstairs to the kitchen. Liz had poured her cup and handed the glass pot to Jamison when his cell phone rang. Liz started to walk away, stopping suddenly when she heard the glass pot hit the tile floor.

She whirled around. Jamison stood still, his phone in one hand and his other empty. Shards of glass and spilled coffee surrounded him.

"Jamison?" She started back toward her boss.

"There's a bomb in my office." He spoke without emotion. "It's set to go off in fifteen minutes."

## Chapter Three

Detective Sawyer Montgomery arrived just minutes after the bomb squad had disarmed, dismantled and disconnected—she wasn't sure of the technical term—the bomb that had been left in the middle of Jamison's desk. It had taken them eleven minutes to arrive. The longest eleven minutes of Liz's life.

Beat cops had been on the scene within minutes of the 911 call that Liz had made from Jamison's phone after she'd pulled him, his phone and herself from the building. They'd blocked off streets and rousted people from their apartments. OCM's neighbors, many still in their pajamas, had poured from the nearby buildings. Mothers with small children in their arms, old people barely able to maneuver the steps, all were hustled behind a hastily tacked-up stretch of yellow police tape.

Liz had wondered if Detective Montgomery would come. She hated to admit it, but she'd considered calling him. In those first frantic moments before help had arrived, she'd desperately hoped for someone capable. And Detective Montgomery absolutely screamed capable. She doubted the man ever encountered anything he couldn't handle.

But now that he'd arrived, Liz wanted to run. She couldn't decide if she wanted to run to him to seek shelter in his embrace or run far from him to protect herself from his intensity, his questions, his knowing looks.

Liz watched him get out of the car and scan the crowd. He said something to the man who rode with him. Liz knew the exact moment he spotted her. It didn't matter that three hundred yards separated them. Liz felt the shiver run up her arm just as if he'd touched her.

"What the hell happened?" he asked when he reached her.

Liz swallowed, trying very hard not to cry. How ridiculous would that be? No one had been hurt. No one injured. And she hadn't even thought about crying until Detective Montgomery had approached.

"Bomb threat," she said. "Actually, more than a threat, I guess. The bomb squad removed it just a few minutes ago."

"Where was it?"

"In the middle of my boss's desk. In a brown sack." The tears that she'd dreaded sprang to her eyes.

"Hey." Detective Montgomery reached out and touched her arm. "Are you okay?"

He sounded so concerned. That almost made the dam break. "I'm fine, really. Everyone's just been great."

Detective Montgomery frowned at her, but he didn't let go. The most delicious heat spread up her arm.

"Come over here." He guided her toward the curb.

"Okay." Whatever he wanted. As long as she didn't have to think. Because then she'd think about it, the bomb and the look on Jamison's face. She'd remember the pure panic she'd felt as they'd run from the building.

He pulled his hand away, and Liz felt the immediate loss of heat all the way to her stomach, which was odd since his hand had been nowhere near her stomach. He unbuttoned his suit coat, took it off and folded it. He placed it on the cement curb. "Why don't you sit down?" he suggested, pointing at his coat.

"I can sit on cement," she protested.

"Not and keep those…short pants clean," he said. His face turned red. "I know there's a word for them, but I can't think of it right now."

He was smokin' hot when he was serious and damn cute when he was embarrassed. It was a heck of a combination. "They're called capri pants."

He smiled. "It might have come to me."

Oh, boy. She sat down. She knew she needed to before she swooned. "I'm sure it would have, Detective Montgomery."

"Sawyer," Detective Montgomery said. "Just Sawyer is fine."

Liz nodded. The man was just being polite. After all, in a span of less than forty-eight hours, their paths had crossed three times. They weren't strangers any longer. She was sitting on his coat. "Liz is fine, too," she mumbled.

"Liz," he repeated.

She liked the way the *z* rolled off his tongue. She liked the way all the consonants and the vowels, too, for that matter, rolled off his tongue. It was a molten chocolate center bubbling out of a freshly baked cake. Smooth. Enticing.

Maybe he could read her the dictionary for the next week.

"I need to ask you some questions," he said.

She wasn't going to get a week. "Sure." Why the heck not? Together they sat on the faded gray cement, hips close, thighs almost touching. Liz wanted to lean her head against his broad shoulder but knew that would startle the hell out of him.

She settled for closing her eyes. It seemed like a lifetime ago that she'd crawled out of bed and caught the five-o'clock bus.

"Sawyer?"

Liz opened her eyes. The man who had been with Sawyer when he'd arrived now stood in front of the two of them.

He was an inch taller and probably ten pounds heavier than Sawyer. He had the bluest eyes she'd ever seen.

Was the sky raining gorgeous men?

"What did you find out?" Sawyer spoke to the man.

"Bomb, all right. Big enough that it would have done some damage. Quick to shut down. Looks like they wanted to make it easy for us."

Sawyer didn't say anything.

"Who are you?" Liz asked.

The man's face lit up with a broad smile showing perfect teeth. "I'm Detective Robert Hanson. My partner has no manners. Otherwise, he'd have introduced us."

"I'm Liz Mayfield."

"I guessed that. It's a pleasure to meet you. I—"

"What else?" Sawyer interrupted his partner.

Detective Hanson shrugged. "We'll get the lab reports back this afternoon. Don't expect much. Guys thought it looked like a professional job."

"Professional?" Sawyer shook his head. "Half the kids in high school know how to build a bomb."

"True." Detective Hanson stared at Sawyer. "Did you get her statement?"

"Not yet," Sawyer said, pulling a notebook and pen from his pocket.

Detective Hanson frowned at both of them. Then he turned toward Liz. "Who got in first this morning?"

"I did," she said. "I got here about five-thirty."

Sawyer looked up from his notebook. "Short night?"

Liz shrugged, not feeling the need to explain.

"Door locked when you got here, Ms. Mayfield?" Detective Hanson asked.

"Yes. After I came in, I locked it again and reset the alarm."

"You sure?"

"I'm usually the first person in. I know the routine."

"Did you see anything unusual once you got inside?"

"No. I went to the kitchen and started a pot of coffee."

"Then what?"

"I heard the front door, and then I thought I heard Jamison's door open. It appears I was right."

"You didn't see anybody?" Detective Hanson continued.

"No. When I left the kitchen, I looked around."

"Then what—"

"You looked around?" Sawyer interrupted his partner.

"Yes."

"You should have called the police."

She frowned at him. His tone had an edge to it. "I can't call the police every time I hear a door."

"You got a threat mailed to your office, and then shots were fired through your window," Sawyer said. "Maybe you should have given that some thought before you decided to investigate."

"Maybe we should keep going." Detective Hanson spoke to Sawyer. "You're taking notes, right?"

Sawyer didn't respond.

"After I *looked around*—" she emphasized the words "—I went down to my office and started working. After Jamison arrived, we came upstairs for coffee."

"What time was that?"

"Almost eight. Jamison's cell phone rang and then…we called 911. That's about it."

"It sounds like you stayed pretty calm. That takes a lot of guts." Detective Hanson smiled at her again.

She smiled back this time. "Thank you."

Sawyer grabbed Robert's arm. "Come on. Let's go. I want to talk to the boss."

Liz stood—so quickly that her head started to spin. She

picked up Sawyer's suit coat, shook it and thrust it out to him. "Don't forget this," she said.

He reached for it, and their fingers brushed. The fine hairs on her arm reacted with a mind of their own. What the heck was going on? She'd never ever had this kind of physical reaction to a man. Especially not one who acted as if he might think she was an idiot.

Sawyer jerked his own arm back. "I'll…uh…talk to you later," he said. Great. She had him tripping over his own tongue.

Sawyer got twenty feet before Robert managed to catch him. "Hang on," he said. "What the hell is wrong with you?"

Sawyer shook his head. "Just forget it."

"You act like an idiot and think I'm going to forget it?"

"Maybe you've forgotten this. We're here to investigate a crime. We've got a lot of people to talk to. I didn't think it made sense to spend any more time with Liz."

*"Liz,"* Robert repeated.

"Yeah, Liz." Sawyer did his best to sound nonchalant. "She told me I could call her Liz."

"Since when do you hang all over witnesses?"

"I wasn't hanging all over her. She seemed upset. I offered her some comfort. Perhaps you've heard of it. It's called compassion." Sawyer started to walk away.

Robert kept pace. "That wasn't compassion I saw. That was a mating call. What's going on here, partner?"

Sawyer didn't know. Didn't have a clue why he started to unravel every time he got within three feet of Liz. "Liz Mayfield is a material witness to a crime. We had questioned her. I figured we needed to move on."

"That's it?"

"What else could it be?"

Robert looked him in the eye and nodded. "Your timing

sucks. I could have had little Lizzy's phone number in another two minutes."

"Lizzy," Sawyer repeated.

"She's my type."

Sawyer clamped down on the impulse to punch his partner, his best friend for the past two years. "She is *nothing* like your type."

Robert cocked his head. "Really?"

"Yeah. Really."

"I'll be damned." Robert laughed, his face transformed by his smile. "You like her."

"You don't know what you're talking about." Sawyer walked away from his partner.

Robert ran to catch up with him. "You're interested in a witness. Mr. Professional, Mr. I-always-use-my-Southern-manners. This has got to be killing you."

"Liz Mayfield is going to help me get Mirandez. That's my only interest," Sawyer said.

Robert slapped him on the back. "You just keep telling yourself that, Sawyer. Let's go talk to the boss."

When Sawyer and Robert reached Liz's boss, the man held up a finger, motioning them to wait while he finished his telephone call. From the one side of the conversation that Sawyer could hear, it sounded as if the guy was making arrangements to refer his clients on to other sources. After several minutes, the man ended the call and put his smartphone in his pocket.

"Detective Montgomery." The man greeted Sawyer, giving him a lopsided smile. "I have to admit I was hoping there wouldn't be any reason for us to talk again."

Sawyer felt sorry for him. He looked as if he'd just lost his best friend. "This is my partner, Detective Robert Hanson."

"Nice to meet you, Detective Hanson. I'm Jamison Curtiss, the executive director of OCM."

Sawyer watched Robert shake the man's hand, knowing Robert was rapidly cataloging almost everything there was to know about Jamison.

"I understand you got the call this morning, warning you of the bomb," Sawyer said.

"Yes. I'd just gotten to work. It was probably about ten minutes before eight."

"What happened then?"

"Liz and I left the building."

"Then what?" Sawyer prompted the man, reaching into his pocket for his notebook.

"Then I got a second call."

"What?" Sawyer stopped taking notes.

"The second call came in just after they'd found the bomb. Same guy who called the first time. Congratulated me on following directions. Then he told me that unless I closed the doors of OCM, there would be another bomb. I wouldn't know when or where, but there would be one."

"Liz Mayfield didn't say anything about a second call." Sawyer couldn't believe that she'd withheld information like that.

"She doesn't know. I'm not looking forward to telling her."

"Anybody else hear this call?" Not that Sawyer didn't believe the guy. The man looked shaken.

"No. It lasted about ten seconds. Then the guy hung up."

"What are you going to do?" Sawyer asked, keeping one eye on Jamison and casting a quick glance back at Liz. His heart skipped a beat when he didn't see her right away. Then he spied her. She had her back toward him. It took him all of three seconds to realize he was staring at her butt and another five to tear his glance away.

Robert laughed at him. He was quiet about it—just loud

enough to make sure Sawyer heard him. Jamison Curtiss looked confused. Sawyer nodded at the man to continue.

"In the past forty-eight hours," Jamison said, "one of my employees received an anonymous threat. On top of that, my business has been shot at and almost blown up. Whoever is trying to get my attention has it. Unless you can tell me that you know who's responsible, I don't think I have a lot of options."

"We don't know—" Robert spoke up "—but we will. Who has a key to OCM?"

"All the counselors. And our receptionist. Everyone has a slightly different schedule."

"And everybody knows the code to turn off the alarm?" Robert asked.

"Of course."

"Keys to the office doors all the same?"

"Yes."

"Same as to the front door?"

"Yes."

Sawyer and Robert exchanged a look. One key and a code. Child's play for somebody like Mirandez.

"You already gave us a list of employees with their home addresses. I'd like their personnel files, too," Robert said.

Jamison wrinkled his nose. "Is that really necessary?" he asked.

"Yes." Sawyer answered in a manner that made sure Jamison knew it wasn't an option.

"Fine. I'll have them to you by this afternoon."

"Anybody else have a key? A cleaning service, perhaps?"

"We all know how to run a vacuum. We can't afford to pay someone to clean."

"Anybody really new on your staff?"

"No, we've all been working together for years. Liz and Carmen came at about the same time."

"Carmen?" Robert asked.

"Lucky for her, her brother wasn't feeling well this morning. She came to work late." Jamison pointed to the group of counselors gathered across the street. "Carmen Jimenez is the dark-haired woman standing next to Liz."

"My God, she's beautiful," Robert said, then looked surprised that the comment had slipped out. "Sorry," he added.

Jamison shrugged. "That's the reaction most men have. Many of our clients are Spanish-speaking. She's a big asset."

Sawyer studied the two women who stood close together, deep in conversation. Carmen stood half a head shorter, her black hair and darker skin a stark contrast to Liz's blond hair and fair complexion. "Liz and Carmen close?"

"Best friends. We're all like family." Frustration crossed Jamison's face. "I've got to talk to them," he muttered. "They deserve to know what's going on."

Sawyer watched him walk across the street, joining Liz, Carmen and one other woman, who looked about ten years older. He assumed it was Cynthia, the counselor who just worked mornings. He couldn't hear what Jamison told them, but by the looks on their faces, they were shocked, scared and, he thought somewhat ironically, Liz and Carmen looked downright mad.

It took another ten minutes before the group broke up. Jamison walked back to Sawyer and Robert. "Well, they know. I told them that I've already started making arrangements for our current clients to be referred to other agencies. We have a responsibility to these young girls."

Sawyer understood responsibility. After all, he'd made it his responsibility to bring in Mirandez. "I'm going to go talk to Liz," Sawyer said to Robert.

Robert gave Liz and Carmen another look. "I'll go with you," he said.

When Sawyer reached Liz, he realized that Mary Thorton sat on the bench directly behind her. The young girl looked up when Sawyer and Robert approached. She didn't smile, frown or show any emotion at all. She just stared at the two of them.

Sawyer couldn't help staring back. The girl had on a green shirt and a too-tight orange knit jumper over it. With her big stomach, she looked like a pumpkin. Then the dress moved in ripples.

Sawyer remembered the first time he'd felt his baby move. It had rocked his world. He'd first put his hand on his girlfriend's stomach, then his cheek. It had taken another hour for the baby to roll over again, but the wait had been worth it.

Sawyer stuck his hand out toward Carmen Jimenez. "Ms. Jimenez," he said. "I'm Detective Montgomery."

"Good morning," she said.

"This is my partner, Detective Hanson."

Robert reached out his own hand. "It's a pleasure, Ms. Jimenez." Robert smiled at the woman. It was the same smile Sawyer had seen work very well for Robert in the past.

Carmen Jimenez didn't have the reaction that most women had. She nodded politely and shook Robert's hand so briefly that Sawyer wasn't sure that flesh actually touched.

Sawyer turned his attention to Mary, keeping his eyes trained on her face. He didn't want to make the mistake of looking at her baby again. "Mary." He spoke quietly. "Where were you at six o'clock this morning?"

"Sleeping."

"Alone?"

Mary gave him a big smile. "I don't like to sleep alone."

"So, I guess whoever you were sleeping with could verify that you were in bed this morning?"

"I don't know. Maybe."

"Come on, Mary. Surely he or she would know if you'd slipped out of bed."

"Trust me on this, Cop. It wouldn't be a she."

"Didn't think so," Sawyer said. "What's his name?"

"I can't tell you."

The girl's eyes had widened, and Sawyer thought her lower lip trembled just a bit. Liz must have seen it, too, because she sat down next to Mary and wrapped her arm around the girl's shoulders.

Sawyer deliberately softened his voice. He needed Mary. Hated to admit it but he did. "Mary, we can help you. But we need to know what's going on. You need to tell us."

"I don't know anything. You'd need to talk to him."

"Mirandez?"

Mary shook her head and frowned at Sawyer.

"No."

"Who, Mary? Come on, it's important."

She hesitated then seemed to decide. "Well, okay. His name is Pooh."

"Pooh?"

"Yeah. Pooh Bear. He's been sleeping with me since I was six."

He heard a laugh. Sawyer whirled around, and Robert suddenly coughed into his hand. Carmen, her dark eyes round with surprise, had her fingers pressed up against her lips. Sawyer looked at Liz. She stared at her shoes.

Damn. He could taste the bitter metal of the hook. The girl had baited her pole, cast it into the water and reeled him in. It was all he could do not to flop around on the sidewalk.

"Funny," he said. "Hope you're still laughing when you're sitting behind bars, waiting for a trial."

Liz stood up and jerked her head toward the right. "May I speak to you in private, Detective?"

Sawyer nodded and walked across the street. When he stopped suddenly, Liz almost bumped into him. She was close enough that he could smell her scent. It was a warm, sticky day already, but she smelled fresh and cool, like a walk through the garden on a spring night.

"Don't threaten her," Liz warned. "If you're going to charge her with something, do it. Otherwise, leave her alone. This can't be good for her or the baby."

Sawyer took a breath and sucked her into his lungs. As crazy as it seemed, it calmed him. "She's a little fool."

"She's a challenge," Liz admitted.

Sawyer laughed despite himself. "Paper-training a new puppy is a challenge."

Liz smiled at him, and he thought the world tilted just a bit.

"I'll talk to her," Liz said.

"How? Isn't she being referred on?"

Liz glanced over her shoulder, as if making sure no one was close by. "I'm going to keep seeing her. She needs me."

"Your boss is closing shop."

"I know. Carmen and I already discussed it. We'll see clients at my apartment."

Calm disappeared. "Are you nuts?"

She lifted her chin in the air.

He pointed a finger at her. "You received a threat. Which may or may not have anything to do with the shooting. Which may or may not have anything to do with today's bomb. Which may or may not have anything to do with Mirandez or Mary or the man in the moon. What the hell are you thinking?"

"I have to take the chance."

She'd spoken so quietly that Sawyer had to lean forward to hear her. "Why?" The woman had a damn death wish.

"I just have to," she said.

Was it desperation or determination that he heard in her tone? All he knew for sure was that nothing he could say

was going to change her mind. "When? When are you starting this?" he asked.

"Mary's coming to see me tomorrow."

Great. That gave him twenty-four hours to figure out how
to save them both.

## Chapter Four

Liz's small apartment seemed smaller than usual after she set up shop at the kitchen table and Carmen took the desk in the extra bedroom. Girls came and went, and while the surroundings were different, the conversations were much the same as if they had occurred in a basement on the South Side.

It was late afternoon when Carmen made her way to the kitchen. "I thought Detective Montgomery might have a stroke yesterday." She took a swig from her water bottle. "He looked like he wanted to wring your neck."

Liz laughed and reached for her coffee cup. She took one sip and dumped the rest down the drain. No coffee was better than cold coffee. "He thinks we're idiots."

"He might be right." She hesitated. "What time was Mary's appointment?" she asked softly.

Liz looked at the clock. "Three hours ago."

"Did you call her?"

"Four times."

Carmen didn't say anything. Finally, she sighed. "There's something very wrong here."

"I know. I just don't know what it is." She ran a hand through her hair. "Are you done for the day?"

"I am. I could stay with you."

"Don't you dare. Your brother is still sick. Go home. Pick up some chicken-noodle soup for him on the way."

"You're sure?"

Liz nodded.

"Okay. I'll call you tomorrow."

Liz watched her friend leave. She waited fifteen minutes before trying Mary's cell phone again. It rang and rang, not even going to voice mail. She tried her three more times in the evening before finally giving up and going to bed.

She woke up the next day, tried Mary, didn't get an answer and finally admitted to herself that she needed help. Carmen was right. Something was very wrong.

Liz called Sawyer. He answered on the second ring.

"This is Liz Mayfield. Mary had an appointment yesterday, but she didn't show or call. I'm worried about her."

She wasn't sure, but she thought she heard him sigh.

"Can't the police do anything?" she asked. "She's just a kid."

"I'll put the word out to my contacts. If anybody sees her, they'll call."

"What about a missing-person report? Should I do one of those?"

"You can." Sawyer didn't think it would hurt but he doubted it would help much. Every day there were lots of teenagers reported missing. Most showed up a few days later safe and sound, sure that they'd taught their parents a thing or two. The true runaways usually called home a couple weeks later, once their money had run out. The smart ones anyway. The dumb ones slipped into a life of prostitution that killed them. Even those who were still technically breathing, working the streets each day, were as good as dead.

Fluentes had made contact late the night before. He had heard that Mirandez had slipped out of town but didn't have specifics. Sawyer thought it likely that Mary had gone with him. For all he knew, the two of them were hiding out in some fancy hotel somewhere, living off room service, enjoying all the benefits that drug money could buy.

"Do you think we should check the hospitals?" Liz asked.

"Probably a good idea. Hell, maybe she had her baby."

"I doubt it. Mary's scared to death of labor. I think she'd call me."

If she could. But maybe Mirandez had put the screws to that. "Are you this tight with all your clients?" Sawyer asked.

"No. But Mary really doesn't have anybody else."

"She has Mirandez," Sawyer said.

"He must have opted out. Maybe he's afraid of blood?"

"Only of seeing his own," Sawyer said. "What about her family? Anybody around here that she'd stay with?"

"Her mother died several years ago. I've met her father. He kicked her out when he found out about the pregnancy. I tried to reason with him, but it was no use. Something along the lines of she's made her bed, now let her lie in it."

His parents had been furious when he'd come home and confessed that he'd gotten his girlfriend pregnant. His mom had cried. His dad had left the house for four hours. But then he'd come home, quietly conferred with his wife, then the two of them sat Sawyer down so that they could discuss what he intended to do about the situation.

He'd wanted to marry Terrie. He found out it didn't much matter what he wanted. Terrie's parents refused to even consider the idea. He'd been the poor kid from the wrong side of the tracks. They'd wanted more for their daughter.

Sawyer had been standing at his son's freshly dug grave when Terrie's father had confessed that not allowing his daughter to marry Sawyer had been a mistake. Sawyer hadn't even responded. Sawyer knew the man thought he could have pulled Terrie back from the drugs that crushed both her body and mind.

Sawyer knew better. He hadn't been able to help Terrie. A marriage license wouldn't have helped him wrestle her away from the cruel grip of addiction. He'd believed Terrie when she'd promised to quit the drugs. In doing so, he'd failed her. That haunted him. He'd failed his helpless son. That had rocked his soul, causing it to crack and bleed.

"She have any friends?" Sawyer asked.

"She talked about a couple girlfriends. But I never met them."

"Okay. Then I guess we wait. See if something comes up."

"There is one place we might check," Liz said. "Mary mentioned a children's bookstore that she liked. Said she spent a lot of time there, looking through books."

"Got a name?"

"I've got an address. I wrote it down. I had planned on finding it and picking out a baby gift." She opened her purse, pulled out the slip of paper and read it to him.

He whistled softly. "Are you sure that's right?"

"Yes. Mary raved about this store. She said Marvis, the owner, was really cool. It's not an area I'm familiar with."

"I'd hope not," Sawyer mocked. "I don't think there're a lot of bookstores in that neighborhood. There are, however, a lot of really great crack houses. I'll go check it out and let you know."

"You're kidding, right?"

He didn't answer.

"Look, Sawyer. You need Mary. I'm the best link you have to her. But if you cut me out—if you even think about leaving me behind—that's the last information I'll share with you."

Sawyer counted to ten. "To interfere with a police investigation is a crime. To willfully withhold evidence is a crime."

"You'd have to prove it first."

Sawyer almost laughed. He'd used his best I'm-a-hard-ass-cop voice. The one that made pimps and pushers shake. But she didn't even sound concerned. "What about your clients?"

"I'll call Carmen. We both had a light day today, so she should be able to cover my clients. She can meet them at a coffee shop near OCM."

"Fine. Be ready in twenty minutes."

Sawyer hung up the phone. He ran his fingers across the stack of manila folders that had been delivered late last night, hot out of the filing cabinets of OCM. Personnel files. Liz Mayfield's file.

He sifted through the pile. When he found hers, he flipped it open. Copies of tax forms. Single with zero exemptions. Direct-deposit form. Emergency-contact form. Harold and Patrice Mayfield, her parents. They had a suburban area code.

He set those papers aside. Next was her résumé. With plenty of detail.

He scanned the two-page document. The label Ph.D. jumped out at him. Liz had a doctorate degree in psychology from Yale University. Up until a few years ago, she'd worked for Mathers and Froit. The name meant nothing to him. He read on. She'd been a partner, responsible for billing out over a half million a year. That was clear enough. She'd been in the big time.

But she'd left that all behind for OCM. Why? With a sigh, Sawyer closed the file. He stood up and snatched his keys off the desk. He almost wished he'd never looked. Even as a kid, he'd been intrigued by puzzles.

He opened his car door just as Robert pulled his own vehicle into the lot. He waited while his friend parked.

"I've got a lead on Mary Thorton," he said when Robert approached.

"Need me to go with?"

"No. It's probably nothing. The personnel files are on my

desk. Spend your time on them. Maybe the connection to OCM isn't Mary. Maybe it's something else."

WHEN SAWYER AND LIZ pulled up to the address, Sawyer started to laugh. A dry chuckle.

Liz looked at the slip of paper and then checked the numbers hanging crooked on the side of the old brick building. There was no mistake. Mary's bookstore was the Pleasure Palace. Brown shipping paper covered the front windows. "What do you think?" she asked.

"I think it's not a Barnes & Noble," he said, smiling at her.

"Let's get this over with," she said, opening her car door.

Sawyer caught up with her fast. "Stay behind me," he instructed. "It's too early for the drug dealers or the prostitutes to be doing business, but there's no telling what else lurks around here."

Liz slowed her pace and let him take the lead. He pushed the door open with his foot. "Also, no telling where people's hands have been that turned that handle," he said almost under his breath.

There were magazines everywhere. Women, their bodies slick with oil, in every pose imaginable. Men with women, women with women, women with dogs. Where the magazines ended, the ropes, chains and harnesses took up.

"I don't believe this." Sawyer let out a soft whistle and pointed.

There, surrounded by DVDs, handcuffs, and plastic and rubber appliances in all shapes and sizes, was a table piled high with kids' books. They were used but in good shape.

Sawyer picked one off the pile. It was the familiar Dr. Seuss book. "I hate green eggs and ham," he said, "Sawyer, I am."

"You think this is funny, don't you?" Liz hissed.

"It's hilarious. It's worth the price of admission."

"There was no admission."

"Trust me on this. There's always a price. We just don't know what it is yet."

"Hello." A voice sang out from the corner.

"But we're just about to find out," Sawyer whispered.

A woman, almost as tall as Sawyer and pleasantly plump, wearing a flowing purple pantsuit floated toward them. She had big hair and bright red lipstick. "Welcome to the Pleasure Palace. I'm Marvis. May I help you find something? A nice DVD perhaps? Or we have some brand-new battery-operated—"

"We're trying to find a book for our friend," Sawyer interrupted. He nodded at the table.

"A children's book?"

"Yeah."

"Well, you've come to the right place. Everything is half-off the cover price. All of these belonged to my grandchildren. They are in good shape. The books, that is." Marvis laughed at her own joke, her double chin bouncing. "Not that my sweet babies aren't fit as a fiddle, too. They can run circles around me."

It would be a fair amount of exercise just getting around Grandma Marvis. Liz caught Sawyer's eye and knew he was thinking the same thing.

"There are over two hundred books here. Every one of my eight grandkids could read before they were five."

"Our friend comes here all the time. She's about five-three, fair skin, freckles, blondish-red hair and pregnant." Sawyer pretended to browse through the pile, all the while keeping an eye on the door.

"Let me think." The woman tapped her polished pink fingernail against her lips.

Sawyer walked over to the counter. He picked the top

DVD off the rack. He looked at the price and pulled a fifty out of his pocket.

"Oh, now I remember. Mary, right?" The woman's doubled chin tucked under when she smiled.

"That's the one."

"Wonderful girl. Loves her books. Always takes one of the classics." She waved her hand toward the end of the table. "Last time she was here, she got *Little Women.* Said she hoped that if she had a daughter she'd be as pretty as Winona Ryder."

"When was she in last?" Sawyer asked.

"It had to have been at least a week ago. I was telling Herbert, he's my man friend, just yesterday that I bet she had her baby. What did she have? She was carrying it so low, I couldn't help but think it was a boy."

"No baby yet. In fact," Sawyer said as he pulled a book off the children's table and threw another twenty at the woman, "if she happens to stop by, would you tell her to call Liz?"

"I'll do that. You all have a nice day. Are you sure I can't interest you in something? We've got a whole new line of condoms. Cartoon characters."

"No thanks." Sawyer literally pulled Liz out of the store and back to the car. He unlocked her side, threw the merchandise in the backseat and got in on the driver's side. He started to drive away without another word.

"I wonder if they come in an assorted box," Liz said.

Sawyer almost ran the car into a light pole.

Not that he needed to worry about causing an unexpected pregnancy. A quick trip to his physician ten years ago had taken care of that. But there were other good reasons to wear protection. With a woman like Liz Mayfield in his bed, he'd probably be hard-pressed to remember that. He'd want her, all of her, without anything to separate the two of them. He'd want—

"Hey, are you all right?" she asked. "You look a little pale."

Sawyer whipped his eyes back to the road. In another minute, she'd start to analyze him. If she found out what he was thinking, she'd probably jump out of the car. "I'm fine," he said.

"So, now where?" she asked.

"I'm taking you home."

"We can't just give up."

"I'm not giving up. But until a clue turns up, we wait. Maybe Mary will get smart and call you."

"You're determined to think the worst of her, aren't you?"

"She's up close and personal with a drug dealer. It's hard to think of her as Mother Teresa."

"Why don't you try thinking of her as a mixed-up, scared, lonely kid?"

"I can't do that." He risked a quick glance at her.

Liz folded her arms across her chest and stared straight ahead. When she spoke, he had to strain to hear her.

"You need to try harder," she said.

He tried. Every damn day he tried. Tried to rid the streets of scum. Tried to arrest just one more of the human garbage that preyed on young bodies and souls. She had no idea how hard he tried. Just like she had no idea that he wanted her more than he'd wanted a woman in years. Maybe ever. And that, quite frankly, scared the hell out of him.

Yeah, he needed to try harder. He needed to keep his distance, needed to remember that getting Mirandez was the goal. Not getting into Liz Mayfield's pants or letting her get into his head.

LIZ WASHED HER DISHES, cleaned her bathroom, sorted some old photographs and even managed to force down a peanut-butter sandwich. She went through all the motions of a regular life. But what she really did was wait for Mary's call.

When the phone finally rang at seven o'clock, she jumped off her couch, ran to the kitchen and managed to stub her toe on the way.

She tried to keep the disappointment out of her voice when Jamison greeted her. "Liz, I talked to Carmen late this afternoon," he said. "I understand that Mary was a no-call, no-show yesterday."

Jamison would understand her worry. She knew she could confide in him. But she couldn't bring herself to utter the words. To somehow give credence to the fact that Mary might be in trouble. That Mary might be, at this very moment, crying out for help, but there would be no one around to hear. If she said it, it could be true.

"You know how these kids are. I'm sure I'll hear from her soon."

"I hope you're right," he said. "I don't know how much help this is, but I did get a lead on Mary that you can pass on to Detective Montgomery."

"What?"

"I reviewed some case files today, and I saw a note that one of my girls had heard about OCM from Mary Thorton. They met at a club."

"What's the name of it?"

"Jumpin' Jack Flash. I guess they have a dance contest every Tuesday night. The women don't pay a cover, and all the drinks are two bucks. It's somewhere on the South Side, on Deyston Street."

Liz knew just where it was. She and Sawyer had passed it this morning on their way to the bookstore. And today was Tuesday.

"He might want to check it out. From what I understood

from my client, it's a real hangout for the young crowd. I had thought about trying to put a few brochures there."

His business, her life.

"Thanks for the tip, Jamison."

"You'll tell Detective Montgomery?"

"I will. Thanks, Jamison." Liz hung up and dialed Sawyer. After four rings, his voice mail came on. "Hi, Sawyer," she said. "I've got a tip on Mary. It's a dance club on Deyston. Call me, okay?"

She waited an hour. She'd tried his line again. When voice mail picked up again, she pressed zero. A woman answered. Detective Montgomery was not in. Was it an emergency? Did she want to page him?

She almost said yes but realized he could be in the middle of trouble. The man had a dangerous job. He didn't need to be interrupted.

She'd just go there by herself, look around and ask a few questions. She'd only stay a short while. Then she could report back to Sawyer. It would probably be better if he wasn't there anyway. He'd do his tough-guy cop routine and scare away any of the girls who might know Mary.

Liz had learned a lot about teenage girls in the past three years. When they got scared, they clammed up. She didn't want the girls circling the proverbial wagons and making it impossible to find Mary.

Liz ran back to her closet and started sorting through her clothes. Business suits or jeans. Old life, new life. She didn't have much in the middle. But tonight, she needed a young, nonestablishment look. It took her twenty minutes to find something that might work. She pulled the short, tight black skirt on, hoping like heck that she wouldn't have to sneeze. The zipper would surely break. Then she put on a black bra and topped if off with a sheer white shirt that had come with one of her swimsuits. She left her legs bare and stuck her feet into high-heeled, open-toed black sandals.

She teased and sprayed her hair, put on three times the amount of makeup she normally wore and walked her body through a mist of perfume. For the finishing touch, she applied two temporary tattoos, one on her breast, just peeking over the edge of her bra, and the other on the inside of her thigh, low enough that it would show when she crossed her legs. She'd remembered them at the last minute. They'd come in a box of cereal. One was a snake and the other a flag. Not exactly what she'd have chosen but better than nothing. Every girl she met had some kind of tattoo or body piercing.

When she got finished and looked in the mirror, she wasn't too dissatisfied with the effort. She didn't look eighteen, but she thought she could pass for her mid-twenties. At least they might not guess she was thirty-two—so far into adulthood, from their perspective, that she couldn't possibly even remember what it was like to be young.

She grabbed a small black purse, stuck her cell phone in it as well as two hundred bucks. She remembered Sawyer's advice from earlier in the day. Everything had a price. She needed to be prepared to pay for information.

She waved down a cab and ignored the guy's look when she told him the address. Thirty minutes later, when he pulled up to the curb, she sat still for a minute, for the first time wondering if she had made a big mistake.

Music poured out of the small, old building. Ten or fifteen teens gathered around the door, lounging against the cement walls. Everybody had a cigarette and a can of beer. More boys than girls. And the few girls who were there were clearly taken. One straddled a boy who sat on a wooden chair. He had his hand up her shirt. Another girl, plastered from lips to toes to her boy, his hands possessively curled around her butt, almost blocked the doorway.

"You getting out, lady?" The cab driver raised one eyebrow at her. "I don't like sitting still in this neighborhood."

Liz swallowed. This morning, the neighborhood had looked gray. Gray buildings, gray sidewalk. The sky had even seemed a little gray, as if it were a reflection of the street below. But tonight, the street seemed black and purple and red. Violent and passionate, the colors of sex and sin. Firecrackers popped, music blasted, the air almost sizzled.

"Yes, I'm getting out." Liz threw a twenty at the driver and stepped from the car.

# Chapter Five

"Oh, baby, I do like blondes." The voice came from her far left. Liz couldn't see him until he stepped away from the corner of the building. He looked older than the other teens, probably in his early twenties. He cocked a finger at her. "Come here. Let's see if they really do have more fun."

A couple of the other teens pushed each other around, laughing, but nobody else said anything. Liz ignored them all and walked into the club.

If it had been loud outside, it was mind-blowing inside. It made her head hurt. She managed to make her way through the crowd and got up to the bar. She stood next to a group of girls, most of them looking about Mary's age. Where the hell were the police? These kids couldn't be old enough to drink. Liz wanted them all busted but just not until she got the information that she wanted.

"I was talking to you outside, baby."

Liz felt heat crawl up her neck. She turned around. It was Creepy Guy from outside. She knew immediately that ignoring him wasn't going to work.

"I heard you." She smiled at him. "But I got to find my friend before I can have my own fun."

He stared at her breasts. Liz resisted the urge to slap him and tell him to get cleaned up and get a job. "I'll help you, baby. Who you looking for? I know everybody here."

She debated for all of three seconds. "Annie Smith. She likes to dance here."

"Don't know her." The man grabbed her arm and pulled her close. He smelled like cigarettes and cheap rum. "Let's you and me dance."

He stood five inches taller, probably eighty pounds heavier and had wrists twice as big as hers. Liz felt the fear spread from her toes to her head. It didn't matter that he was ten years younger. Age and experience didn't give her an advantage. Brute strength would win every time.

She took her free hand and stroked him under the chin with the back of her fingers. "I'd like that," she said. When he took his free hand and cupped her butt, she forced the smile to stay on her face. "You stay here," she said. "I'm gonna be right over there with those girls. You'll be able to see me." She opened her purse and pulled out a twenty. "Buy me a drink, sugar. Buy yourself one, too."

Then she pulled away from him and edged over to the group of girls that were still gathered just feet away. Several of them turned and stared at her when she joined the group. Then they started talking again as if she wasn't there.

Lord, it was just like high school.

She couldn't wait for them to warm up to her. She had only minutes before the creep at the bar got tired of waiting. She moved around the group, stopping when she stood next to a girl she guessed to be about five months pregnant.

"What do you want?" The girl took another drag off her cigarette.

Liz wanted to rip it away. Didn't she know what that was doing to her baby's lungs?

"I'm looking for Mary Thorton."

The girl looked over both shoulders then started to move away. "Stop, please," Liz pleaded, keeping her voice low.

"My name is Liz, and I think she's in trouble. I want to help her."

"Liz who?"

"Liz Mayfield. I work at Options for Caring Mothers on Logan Street."

Liz saw the flicker of recognition in the young girl's eyes. "You'll get in trouble asking about Mary," the girl advised, her voice low. "She ain't around anyway. She and Dantel went to Wisconsin. She said they were going fishing. Up by Wisconsin Dells."

"Are you sure?" Liz asked, aware that the man from the bar, a drink in each hand, walked toward her.

"That's what she told me. I don't think she wanted to go, but I don't think her boyfriend likes the word *no*."

Liz wanted to hug the young woman. Instead, she winked at her, took a step backward and loudly said, "Hey, if you don't know Annie Smith, you don't need to be such a bitch about it. I just asked a freakin' question."

She turned toward the door, but the guy with the drinks intercepted her before she got five feet. *Damn.* "Oh, thanks," she said and reached for the drink that she had absolutely no intention of sipping. She might be thirty-two and well past the bar scene, but she knew all about date-rape drugs.

Creepy Guy looked her up and down. Then he put his nearly empty glass and her full glass down on the nearest table, grabbed her hand and yanked her out into the sea of bodies. "Let's dance, baby. You can drink later."

The smell of sweat and cheap liquor almost overwhelmed Liz. When the man pulled her close and she could feel his erection, her mind almost stopped working. He had his hands on her butt and his mouth close to her ear.

She thought she might throw up.

Suddenly, the crowd parted and girls started screaming. Twenty feet away, two men were fighting. One had picked up a chair, and the other had a knife. Liz watched as yet another man, holding a beer bottle like a club, stepped into the mix.

Creepy Guy let go of her.

"I gotta pee," Liz said and ran for the bathroom.

There was no damn window in the bathroom. She moved into one of the stalls and grabbed her phone out of her purse. She dialed Sawyer's number. It rang and rang.

"Hey, don't take all day. The rest of us got to pee, too." An angry fist pounded on the door.

"Just a minute," Liz said. Sawyer's voice mail kicked on. Liz flushed the toilet so that she could talk. "Sawyer, I need help. I'm at 1882 Deyston." She disconnected that call and had just started to dial 911 when the door to the stall was kicked open.

"Everybody out," a female cop yelled at her. "Put your hands in the air and walk to the door."

Liz wanted to put her arms around the woman and hug her. But the gun pointed at her told her that wouldn't be appreciated.

Liz walked out into the club area. Some of the grayness from the daytime had eased back in. The lights had been turned on, and the music had been turned off. There were at least ten cops, with more pouring through the open door. Within minutes, the cops paired off, breaking the group into smaller groups. Everybody had to empty their pockets, their purses. A female officer patted Liz down, looking for weapons. She didn't care.

Liz didn't even care when she had to sit on the dirty floor, her hands on top of her head. Anything was better than dancing with that man, his erection pressed up against her, his hands grabbing at her butt. Thank God he hadn't tried to kiss her. Even now, the thought of it made her gag.

She sat quietly. The girl next to her cried; the boy on the other side screamed obscenities at the cops who stood around the perimeter of the room. Liz scanned the area for the pregnant girl who'd given her the info, but she was nowhere to be seen. Somehow, she'd managed to slip out.

Liz tried to remember every cop show she'd ever watched. When did people get fingerprinted? When was the mug shot taken? Would she get to make a phone call before or after all that?

Who the heck would she call? Sawyer hadn't been at his desk. She couldn't ask Carmen to come down to the police station at eleven o'clock on a Tuesday night. The only person she could call was Jamison. He'd have a cow, but then he'd come.

A minute later, when Sawyer, with his partner Robert on his heels, came through the doors, she realized that Jamison wasn't the only one likely to have a cow.

Sawyer literally skidded to a stop. He didn't say a word. He couldn't.

"Damn," Robert said.

"Hi," Liz said.

"What the hell are you doing here?" Sawyer demanded. God, he'd been scared. When he'd gotten her messages, he'd driven like a crazy person to the bar, calling Robert on the way. They'd gotten there almost at the same time. When he'd seen more than a dozen squads outside, all kinds of crazy thoughts had entered his head.

Now that he was sure she wasn't hurt, he wanted to wring her little neck. "You came here, looking like *that?*" he said.

She put her chin in the air. "I had to fit in. I couldn't wear my jeans."

"Did you have to dress like a damned hooker?"

He regretted it the minute he said it. But he was scared. He hadn't been there to protect her. What if she'd gotten hurt? Raped? Killed?

"I didn't think a three-piece suit would fit in," she said.

"You didn't think. Period."

If anything, she put her nose a bit higher in the air. "I called you. I tried to reach you."

"You left a stupid message. Page me. That's why I leave the number."

"I didn't want to bother you," she said.

"Bother me?" This woman drove him crazy. "All you've been is a bother since the day I met you."

"Look, Sawyer," Robert interjected. "There's no harm done. She's fine. We're all fine. Don't be an idiot about this."

Sawyer rubbed a hand across his face. He could see the pain in Liz's pretty green eyes. It was hurt he'd caused.

He took a deep breath. When he spoke, he raised his voice just enough that Liz could hear but that the rest of the people in the room would have to make up their own story. "I'm sorry, Liz. I'm more sorry than you can imagine. I was worried and…and I'm not handling this well." His voice cracked at the end.

"I want to go home," Liz said. "Will you take me?"

He felt the weight of the world lift off his shoulders. "Yeah, I'd be glad to." He looked at Robert and nodded his head at the officer who seemed to be in charge. "Can you…"

"No problem. I'll give our boys the CliffsNotes version so that they understand why she's making a quick exit. Get going."

Sawyer nodded, wrapped an arm around her and walked her out of the bar.

He wished he had a coat, something that he could throw over her, cover up some skin. What in the hell had she been thinking?

Once inside his car, Sawyer kept his hands firmly wrapped around the steering wheel, afraid that he might just reach out and shake her. Of course, once he touched her, he'd be toast. It would all be over for him. He'd end up kissing and touching her and maybe more if she didn't have the good sense to stop him.

It would be wrong. She deserved better than what he had to offer. Which was nothing. Liz Mayfield was young, pretty and someday would make some man a fine wife. They'd have pretty babies, and God willing, she and her husband would see them grow up, go to their first baseball game, drive a car, go to college, have a life.

He'd thought he'd had it. Then he'd lost it. His baby's precious body had grown cold in his arms. The nurses, the professionals who were used to saying the words *baby* and *death* in the same sentence, let him be. They walked around his rocking chair, careful to keep their voices down, their eyes never quite meeting his.

Much wiser now, he knew what he had. He had his work, his career. He made important arrests that got scum off the streets. He made a difference every day. That was more than some people had in a lifetime. It had to be enough for him.

He'd been half out of his mind with worry when he'd gotten the two voice mails from her. He'd listened to the first and realized that she intended to go to Deyston Street and then the second; when he'd heard the panic in her voice and knew she was scared and possibly hurt, his heart had almost stopped.

It had been a huge relief when he saw her. And then he'd turned stupid. The worry eating at his soul had burst from his mouth, and he'd hurt her. He regretted that. But she needed to understand how big of a mistake she'd made. For her own sake. She didn't understand how violent, how cruel, how humiliating the street—and those who called the street their home—could be.

He would take her back to her apartment, and they would talk. He wouldn't yell, and he wouldn't accuse. It would be a civil conversation, one adult to another. He'd make her understand that she needed to let the police look for Mary. That she needed to stop seeing OCM's clients at her apartment. Then he'd leave.

Sawyer found a spot near the front of Liz's apartment building. "I'd like to come in," he said. He was proud that he sounded so calm, so reasonable. See, he could do this.

"I'm not sure that's a good idea."

"We should talk. I'd be more comfortable talking in your apartment." Wow. *He* should be the shrink.

He waited until she nodded before he quickly got out of the car. Yep, everything would be fine. They'd have a nice quiet conversation, and he could leave, knowing that she'd be safe.

He walked around the car and opened Liz's door. Oh, hell. From this angle, her legs went on forever. She had them crossed, one sexy, small foot, with painted red toenails, dangling over the other. Tanned legs, absolutely silky smooth. Round knees, firm thighs and a…a snake. No way! It couldn't be! He squatted down next to the open door, and with his index finger, he tapped against the tattoo.

"What the hell is this? Are you nuts?"

"Sawyer, it's just…"

"It's not just a tattoo," he yelled. "You have the most beautiful, incredibly sexy legs." He pulled his hand back and rubbed his temple, as if he suddenly had a very bad headache. "How could you even think about getting a tattoo? And a snake. Were you drunk on your butt or what?"

"Stop yelling. My neighbors will call the cops. I'm not dealing with that again tonight."

She unbuttoned the top three buttons on her shirt. "It's a rub-on. See? Just like this one."

He did not intend to look. There was really no need. But he couldn't stop himself. And when she stuck two slim fingers in her mouth, wet them with her tongue and then rubbed her breast, blending the stars and stripes of the American flag, his knees almost gave out.

## Chapter Six

"You need to stop doing that," he warned.

"But…" She looked up at him, confusion clear in her green eyes. "I just wanted you to see—"

"I see. I don't need to see another thing. Let's go." He turned away, not looking as she maneuvered those long legs out of the car.

"They came out of a cereal box," she said.

He'd never be able to eat his Cheerios again. "Fine. Let's not talk about tattoos anymore, okay?" He motioned for her keys, and she handed them to him. He unlocked the apartment door. He held up his palm, stopping her. He went inside, took a quick look around the apartment, and when he came back, he pulled her inside and shut the door.

"You and I are going to talk. But first, go take a shower. I'll make coffee."

"I don't really drink coffee at night. I'd prefer some tea. Something herbal. It's in the cupboard."

Herbal. He needed strong, get-a-grip caffeine and she wanted herbal. "Fine. Whatever. Just get that stuff off your face and get rid of those tattoos."

He made the stupid tea and tried not to think about how she'd look in the shower, the water sliding over her slim, firm body. The woman truly had an incredible shape. He'd appreciated it before, but now that he'd seen a bit more of it, he might have moved into the worship stage.

He had already finished one cup of tea when she came back to the kitchen. Her long hair, looking a bit darker when wet, was pulled back in a loose braid. She had on a T-shirt, a pair of jogging shorts and white socks. No makeup. Not a speck. She looked about sixteen. He felt better. He wouldn't be tempted to stick his hands up her shirt if she didn't look legal.

"Here's your tea."

"Thanks."

She sat on the stool next to the kitchen counter and took dainty little sips. Neither of them said a word for a few minutes. When she did speak, she surprised him.

"I did a stupid thing tonight," she said.

Yeah, that was exactly what he'd intended to tell her.

"Something bad could have happened, and it would have been my own fault."

Right. That about summed it up. Why didn't it give him more pleasure to hear her say it? To have her admit that she was out of her league?

"I didn't want to miss meeting Mary's friends. I didn't stop to think about all the other people who would be there."

He hated—absolutely hated—seeing her this beaten. "Just forget it," he said. "It's over."

And then she started to cry. She might sip daintily, but she cried loud and rough. Her nose got red, big tears slid down her cheeks, her shoulders shook and she made choking sounds. Knowing it was stupid, knowing he'd probably regret it, he walked around the counter and wrapped his arms around her.

"Now, now." He tried to comfort her. "You had a tough night. Everything will be better in the morning."

"I hate being a girl. I hate being smaller, shorter, weaker. I hate being afraid."

The muscles in his stomach tightened.

"Did somebody threaten you?" He pulled back just enough so that he could look her in the eye.

"No. It's nothing. I'm just tired."

She was lying. "Did somebody touch you tonight?" He felt a burn. It started in the pit of his stomach, then exploded into his arms and legs, making him shake. He was going to kill the bastard.

She shrugged her shoulders, trying to dismiss him. He stopped her. "I told you once. Don't lie to me. Don't ever lie to me."

She gave one last sniff and lifted her chin in the air. "When I got out of the cab, there were a bunch of teenagers outside of the building. One of them said something. He looked a bit older than the rest, maybe twenty or so. I just ignored him. But when I got inside, I couldn't shake him."

"What did he do?" He didn't want to know. He didn't want to hear it.

"He wanted to dance."

"Okay."

"I tried to get out of it. He was too strong. I couldn't get away without making a scene. I'd gotten the information I needed. All I wanted to do was get out of there without a bunch of people wondering who I was and why I was there. I think he might have been high on something. He seemed just on the edge of being out of control."

She'd gotten information about Mary. He didn't care. "What did he do to you?"

"He pulled me close and I could feel…him." She blushed but recovered quickly. "I could feel him poking into me and I got scared. I was in a strange place, I didn't know a soul and he outweighed me by at least eighty pounds." She blinked her eyes, where tears still clung to her thick lashes. "Then there was a fight. I guess that's why the cops came. Anyway, I told him I had to pee and I ran to the bathroom. When the cops came, I almost hugged them."

He pulled her close, held her next to his heart and bent his mouth very close to her ear. "I'm sorry that happened to you. I'm sorry he touched you. I'm sorry he scared you. But you need to forget it. You're never going to see him again."

She moved even closer, and her curves suddenly filled his hands. Her heat warmed him. She kissed the side of his neck.

*Let it be enough,* he prayed. *Let it be enough.* But he knew it wouldn't. He wanted her mouth, he wanted her hands, he wanted her legs spread apart. He wanted to make love with her for about a day. That might be enough.

"I'm very grateful," she said, making him feel like a lecherous old man. She looked sixteen, and she'd just given him a shy, sweet little kiss and a gracious thank-you. And all he could do was think about pushing her backward, getting her legs hooked over his arms and coming inside of her until one of them passed out.

Then she wrapped her arms around his back and hugged him. He could feel the whole length of her body. It pressed up against him, tempting him. She smelled so good. Sweet and fresh. He bent his head over her wet hair, breathing in the scent of her shampoo. He moved his hands across her back, fingering the bottom of her T-shirt. God help him, he needed to touch her.

He put one hand under her shirt, lightly rubbing her bare back. He moved his fingers over her warm skin, loving the silky feel of her. He moved his hand a bit higher, finding only skin. The woman hadn't put a bra on. Was she crazy? Didn't she have a clue what that did to him, to feel her warm skin, to know that he was just inches away from holding her breast in his hand?

And when she lifted her face and her lips were just inches from his, he went down for the count. He kissed her. Long and slow. And when he slid his tongue into her mouth and she suckled lightly on it, he got instantly hard.

Never taking his mouth away from hers, he moved his hand across her ribs and cupped one breast, loving the feel of the heavy weight, loving the softness, the warmth. He brushed his fingers across her nipple, groaning when she arched her back and pressed her breast more fully into his open hand. He shifted, pressing his hardness against her softness.

She jerked her head back, her eyes wide open.

Her soft, liquid warmth had turned into a hard, solid block of ice.

He was an idiot. A senseless, selfish idiot. She'd already had one man tonight poking into her, causing her to be scared. And now he was doing the same thing. With grim resolution, he pulled away from her, putting a good foot between their bodies.

"I'm sorry," he said. "I can't believe I did that. I…I should be shot."

She laughed. A bit shaky perhaps but it gave him a little hope. "I think that's extreme," she said.

"I'm not so sure. I'm attracted to you," he said. "But you don't have to worry. It would be unprofessional for me to pursue a relationship with you."

She stared at him.

"I'm a cop," he said, reminding both of them. "I'm investigating a murder. I can't do anything to compromise that investigation."

He could tell that she was starting to get it.

"Never mind," Sawyer said, thinking he'd rather be just about anywhere else than explaining to her why he couldn't even think about sleeping with her. "I think I'd better go." He grabbed his keys off the counter.

Liz's braid had flipped over one shoulder, and she played with the wet ends. "Don't you even want to know what I learned about Mary?" she asked, her voice subdued.

Yes. No. Hell, he'd been so far gone that he'd forgotten all about Mary. He moved behind the counter, needing the physical barrier. "What?"

She took a sip of tea. "Mary and Dantel Mirandez are fishing in Wisconsin."

He laughed, glad that he still could. "Sure they are."

Her cheeks turned pink. "I talked to one of Mary's friends tonight. At first, she wouldn't tell me anything. But then I think she decided that I might be able to help Mary."

"Did she say Mary needed help?"

"No, but she acted nervous, like she didn't want to be caught talking about Mirandez or Mary."

"Smart girl. Liz, I can't see Mirandez with a fishing pole. Not unless he'd diced somebody up and was using them for bait."

"You said Mirandez was smart. If he wanted to disappear, doesn't it make sense that he'd go somewhere you'd never think to look?"

"Yeah, but fishing? And anyway, even if I believed it, there has to be at least a thousand lakes in Wisconsin. We'd never find him."

"It's someplace near Wisconsin Dells."

Near Wisconsin Dells. Or The Dells, as all the vacationers called it. One of the detectives he worked with had just taken his family there. He'd called it Little Disney. There were lots of water parks, miniature golf courses and restaurants. Home of the Tommy Bartlett ski show and the boats shaped like ducks that cruised up and down the Wisconsin River.

He couldn't for the life of him see Mirandez at a place

like that. "It just sounds too bizarre," he said, absolutely hating to see the look of disappointment on her face. "Even if he's there, we wouldn't have a clue where to start looking."

"Yes, we do. He's at a cabin. We just have to check out the cabins in the area."

"It's Wisconsin. The state is full of cabins and campgrounds. Even if we know it's around The Dells, it's a big area to search."

She didn't look convinced. "I have to try," she said.

He got a bad feeling in the bottom of his stomach. "You're not trying anything. Wasn't tonight enough of a lesson?"

She swallowed hard, and he felt bad about throwing it in her face. But if that was what it took to keep her safe at home, he didn't feel that bad.

"Yes, tonight sucked. I got hit on by a kid and spent a half hour sitting on a dirty floor. But it's nothing in the grand scheme of things. I have to find Mary."

"The police will find Mirandez. And Mary will be there. We've got a huge amount of manpower out on the street. It's only a matter of time."

"Not if he's fishing."

"Gang leaders do not fish." Sawyer pounded his fist against the kitchen counter.

"You can't be sure of that." Liz started to pace around her apartment. "I don't know what's going on here. I've thought about it for days, and nothing seems to make sense. Well, maybe one thing. That first day we met, after the shooting, you said that it seemed like Mirandez wanted Mary's attention. That he wasn't actually trying to hurt her."

"Right. She's his girlfriend. Maybe he's partial to sleeping in the same bed every night."

"No. It's more than that. I think Mirandez thinks it's his baby."

"You told me it belonged to a student at Loyola."

"Yes. But I think Mary told Mirandez something different."

"Why?"

"Because she's young and alone and probably desperately wanted someone to want both her and the baby."

"Then the Loyola kid was just convenient."

"Perhaps. But he didn't deny that he'd slept with Mary."

"Who knows how many men she slept with?" He hated to be quite so blunt, but Liz needed to stop looking at Mary with rose-colored glasses. She surprised him when she didn't look offended.

"You're right. We don't know. And maybe Mirandez doesn't, either. You said that Mary had been his girlfriend for the past six months. She's eight months pregnant."

Sawyer sat down on one of the counter stools, tapping two fingers against his lips, deep in thought. "So, she's two months along before she ever sleeps with Mirandez. But he doesn't know it."

"Maybe she didn't even know it. But she probably figured it out fast enough. By that time, Mirandez was taking care of her, giving her money, making her feel important."

"So, she doesn't want to walk away from a good thing." Sawyer didn't bother to try to hide his disgust.

"Or she was afraid to try to walk away. Especially once she saw the murder. Maybe that's why Mirandez tried to frighten her. To let her know that he wasn't going to let her walk away."

"Because he loves her?" Sawyer shook his head. "It's possible, I suppose."

"Maybe he wants the baby?" Liz raised an eyebrow.

Sawyer shook his head. "He's a killer. Why would a gang leader, a professional drug dealer, want a baby? And what's so special about this baby? Who knows how many kids he already has running around the city?"

"I don't know. But if I'm right and he does want the baby, then Mary's life isn't worth the price of bubblegum once she gives birth."

Sawyer didn't say anything for a few minutes. "Or maybe she and Mirandez are playing house somewhere, and she doesn't want to be found. She might not be in any danger at all."

"I can't take that chance. Mirandez might be holding her against her will. She's the one person who can send him to jail. Once she has that baby, she's a loose end that he can tie up."

"She should be safe enough for a couple weeks. Didn't you say that the baby wasn't due until September?"

"Babies are known to come early."

"We'll alert every hospital in the state. In Wisconsin, too. Hell, in the whole damn country. If someone comes in matching Mary's description, we'll have her."

"But what if he won't let her go to the hospital?"

"He's a drug dealer, not a doctor." Even Mirandez wouldn't be stupid enough to try to deliver a baby.

"Blood probably doesn't bother him."

Yeah, but delivering a baby? Sawyer had watched the obligatory films in the academy. But in all his years on the police force, he'd never had to deliver a baby. Even before that, when his son had been born, his girlfriend hadn't called until it was all over. He'd raced to the hospital to see his four-hour-old son. He'd barely left the hospital for the next thirteen days. He'd slept and eaten only when he'd been on the verge of falling down. He'd stayed there until they'd taken the body of his son from his arms, leaving him forever alone.

"I gave her a chance to come forward. If she was scared of Mirandez, why didn't she say something?" Sawyer asked.

"I don't know. Maybe she thought that Mirandez would

kill her, too. Maybe she thought Mirandez would rest easy once he found out that she didn't intend to turn him in."

"I don't think he's the type to forget. They don't teach you to turn the other cheek in the hood."

"I don't think she has lots of experience with men like Mirandez."

"No one does. They all die first."

Liz shrugged. "That's why I'm going after her."

No way. Evil surrounded Mirandez. He wouldn't risk letting that evil leak out and touch Liz. "That's not possible. It's a police matter."

"But you said the police are searching in Chicago. They aren't going to find Mirandez or Mary."

"We know Mirandez has dropped out of sight. But we don't have any reason to believe that Mirandez is in Wisconsin. I told you that we have people on the inside. There's been no talk about fishing. He would have told somebody in his organization. And our guys would know."

"I think the girl at Jumpin' Jack Flash told me the truth."

"What was her name?"

Liz blushed. "I didn't ask. I didn't want to scare her. She had dark hair, about shoulder length, with olive-colored skin. Late teens. I'd estimate she was five or six months pregnant."

"Of course."

Liz raised an eyebrow when she heard the bitterness in his voice. "Are you automatically discounting everything she said because she's young and pregnant?"

Young pregnant women lied. His girlfriend had lied to him. Mary had lied. Why wouldn't this one lie? "No. But I don't accept it as gospel."

Liz shook her head, clearly disgusted with him. "I'm going to Wisconsin. She needs me."

"You don't even know where to begin," he protested.

"I'll get a map. I've got some recent photos of Mary. I'll

show them around, and somebody will have seen her. Someone will know where I can find her."

If it was that easy, they wouldn't have a stack of missing-person reports. "It's too dangerous. I can't let you do it." When she opened her mouth to protest, he held up a hand. "I'll ask Lieutenant Fischer to send a few guys north. We'll expand the search. We'll notify both local and state authorities in Wisconsin." It was the best he could do. Probably better than the half-baked lead deserved.

"Thank you. But I'm still going. I have to."

She wasn't going to let him keep her safe. "Mary doesn't deserve this kind of loyalty. She lied to you. She told you that she didn't even know Mirandez. You know that she's been living with him for the past six months. Don't you even care that she looked you in the eye and lied to you?"

"Mary's in a fragile state right now. I'm not sure she's able to make good decisions."

"*You're* not making good decisions," he accused. When she shrugged in return, he knew continued arguing would get them nowhere.

"You should probably go," she said. "I want to get an early start."

"I hope to hell she's worth it," he said as he pulled the door shut behind him.

# Chapter Seven

Sawyer called Lieutenant Fischer from his car, knowing he had a responsibility to give the man any information that might lead to Mirandez's capture. The older man listened, asked a couple questions and agreed it was a long shot. That said, he'd assign a few resources to Wisconsin. They couldn't afford to ignore any lead, no matter how preposterous.

"There's one other thing, Lieutenant," Sawyer said. Now that he'd had a minute to think about Liz going to Wisconsin, he realized that there was one good thing about it. If whoever had sent the threat was serious about it, it got her out of harm's way here.

"Yes."

"Liz Mayfield intends to search, as well. Would you… Could you get the word out? I don't want her getting caught in any cross fire."

Lieutenant Fischer didn't answer right away. When he did, he surprised Sawyer. "We should use Liz Mayfield."

The department didn't use civilians. They weren't trained. They could botch up almost any action, putting officers at risk. "I don't understand, sir."

"You think that Mary Thorton willingly went with Mirandez?"

"I think there's a high probability of that," Sawyer answered. "She's been living with him for months. She didn't turn on him when she had the chance."

"If that's true, she's going to run if she thinks the cops are closing in. Or she's going to tell Mirandez and they'll both run, or there's going to be a bloody battle between Mirandez and us. But if Liz gets close, she may be able to talk to the girl. You said yourself that there seemed to be a really strong bond between the two of them. That if anyone could get to Mary, it would be her."

Sawyer regretted ever having said those words. "Sir, you *cannot* send her after Mirandez. He's a monster. He wouldn't think twice about killing her."

"That's why I'm sending you with her. It's your job to keep her safe. If she gets hurt, I'm going to have the mayor and her boss and God knows who else wanting my head. Stick to her like glue."

There was no damn way. "No."

"Why not?"

He couldn't tell his lieutenant about what had happened in Liz's kitchen, that he'd almost exploded from wanting her. "She's not going to like having me as her shadow."

"Too bad. She doesn't have a choice. Some things just can't be negotiated."

He was a doomed man. "Will you let Robert know where I am?"

"Sure. By the way, I talked to him just a little while ago. He told me that the two of you had sprung Liz from Jumpin' Jack Flash."

Good call on Robert's part. Better to tell the boss rather than let him hear it through the grapevine. "Seemed like the right thing to do," Sawyer said.

"It's fine," his boss said.

Sawyer understood. Lieutenant Fischer wasn't going to worry about the small stuff when he was close to snagging Mirandez.

LIZ FROZE WHEN SHE HEARD the knocking on her front door. In the mirror, she could see the reflection of the digital alarm clock. Eight minutes after four. No one knocked on her door at that time of the morning.

Mary. She spit out the toothpaste, took a gulp of water and grabbed a towel. She wiped her mouth on the way to the door. "Just a minute," she yelled. She wanted to yank the door open but took the extra second to check the peephole. She looked, pulled back, blinked a couple times and looked again.

Sawyer. She twisted the bolt lock to the right, pulled the chain back and opened the door.

"What happened?" she said.

"Can I come in?"

She opened the door wider. "It's Mary, isn't it? Oh, God, is she all right?"

"Liz, calm down. I don't know anything more than I knew last night when I left here."

"Oh." She felt the relief flow through her body. No news wasn't necessarily good news, but it wasn't bad news, either. Swiftly on the heels of the relief came annoyance. "What are you doing here?"

She thought he looked a bit unsure. But that must be her imagination. *Capable* Detective Montgomery didn't do unsure.

"You said you were leaving early." Sawyer gave her a slight smile. "I know you sometimes get up at the crack of dawn. I didn't want to miss you."

"It's four o'clock," she said.

He shrugged his broad shoulders. "I didn't wake you."

No, he hadn't. She'd already showered, dried her hair and packed her bag. In another ten minutes, she'd have been gone.

"Why are you here?" she asked again.

"I'm going with you. To look for Mary."

She backed up a few steps and shook her head. Her tired mind must be playing tricks on her.

"Do you have any coffee made?" Sawyer asked.

"No." She didn't intend to offer him coffee. First of all, the man had kissed her like crazy and then stopped. It was the stopping she was mad about. Then he had compounded his errors by dismissing the notion that she might have gotten a viable lead on Mary. Now he acted as if he had every right to come to her house at four in the morning for conversation and coffee.

He crinkled his nose and pretended to sniff the air. "Funny. That smells like coffee."

She'd been done in by hazelnut beans. "I've got a timer. It must have turned on."

"Great. I could use a cup."

He could pour his own. She intended to go finish packing, and then they would go their separate ways.

"Fine. Cups are on the counter. I've got things to do."

He nodded and pointed at the corner of her mouth. "You've got just a speck of toothpaste there."

Oh, the nerve of this guy. "I was saving it for later," Liz said, her voice dripping with sweetness.

Sawyer laughed. "Good one. You're funny in the morning."

He'd think funny when she left him standing on the curb.

Ten minutes later, Liz walked into the kitchen. Sawyer stood at the counter, drinking out of her favorite cup and eating a piece of toast. "I made you some," he said. "I didn't know if you liked jelly."

"Sawyer." Liz smiled, purposefully patronizing. She felt

calmer now that she'd had a few moments to herself. "This is bizarre. You can't come to my house at four in the morning and have breakfast."

"I packed enough to last a week. I suggest you do the same."

A week? He expected her to spend a week with him?

Liz grabbed for the piece of toast he held out to her. She needed food. She surely had low blood sugar. He couldn't have said *a week*. It would all be better once she'd eaten.

"I did an internet search last night," Sawyer continued, as if he had every right. "I've identified the most likely places."

Likely places? "Sawyer, stop. You're giving me a headache. First of all, when did you have time to do an internet search? You left here just hours ago. Did you sleep at all? And more important, why are you doing this? Last night you didn't seem to think that my information had much value."

"Any lead is better than no lead."

"Well, you can't go with me." She couldn't spend a week with him. Heck, she couldn't spend an hour with him without itching to touch him. Mr. Can't-compromise-the-investigation had no idea that given another two minutes last night, she'd have been all over him. The man had no idea just how much at risk he'd been. The desire had been swift, hot, almost painful.

Throughout the very short night, she'd relived the scene over and over again. By morning, she'd been almost willing to admit that he'd probably done the right thing. There was no need for the little spark between the two of them to grow into a really big flame. With air, a little encouragement and fresh sheets, it could be spontaneous combustion.

They'd both be burned, hurt worse than they could imagine.

Which was ridiculous. Absolutely not necessary. They both wanted Mary. He wanted to use the girl. She wanted to save her. Same goal, different objectives. No common values or mission statement. There was no need to share strategy. Certainly no need to share a car.

"I want to go by myself," she stated.

"No."

Who had died and put him in charge? "You can't stop me."

"I can," he said, suddenly sounding very serious, more like he had the night before. "I'm the lead detective on the case. If you don't cooperate with me, I'll have you arrested for interfering with a police investigation."

"You wouldn't do that," she accused. He just stood there, not blinking, not moving.

"I'll do what I have to do."

"You…you…" she sputtered, unable to find the word that captured her anger. "You cop." It was the best she could do at four in the morning.

He shrugged. "I want Mirandez. Mary's my ticket. She testifies against Mirandez and we get to throw away the key. I haven't made any bones about what I'm trying to do. You think they're in Wisconsin. That's as good a guess as any right now. Are you ready to go?"

She wasn't going anywhere with him. "I'm packed. I'm leaving. Solo. Alone. You can follow me if you want, but we aren't going together."

"That's a waste of gas if we're both going the same way."

He didn't *really* care about wasting gas. "You're afraid that I'm going to warn Mary. You don't trust me."

He looked a little offended. "I trust you. About as much as you trust me."

She didn't trust him one bit. He'd steal her heart and never give it back. She'd be the Tin Man looking for the Wizard.

"I want Mirandez to pay for his crimes," Liz said. "If you're right and Mary can testify against him, I'll do everything I can to persuade her to do so."

"You still refuse to accept that she might be part of this."

"She's not."

"Fine. I'll be the first to say I'm wrong. But if I'm right, I'm going to arrest both of them. Maybe it would be in Mary's best interests if you were with me when I find them."

Mary wouldn't talk to Sawyer. Liz knew that. He was everything she despised. She'd clam up, or worse yet, she'd spout off and probably irritate the hell out of him. She didn't think Sawyer would arrest her out of spite. He wasn't that type of cop or man. No, Sawyer wasn't the wild card. But Mary was. She needed to be there when the two of them met up again.

"All right," she said. "We'll go together. But you'd better not slow me down."

"Don't worry. We'll be there in three hours. Then we start working the river."

"Working the river?"

"Yes. In that area, most of the major campgrounds and resort areas are close to the Wisconsin River. We'll pick a point and then work both sides of the river, north and south. The girl at Jumpin' Jack Flash said he was fishing. He's got to be staying in the area. Could be a tent, a cabin or a damn resort. We'll check them all. If we're going to do this, we do it right."

That seemed like a whole lot of *we*. "Fine." Did she just say *fine?* What was she thinking? "Let's go."

"We can take your car or I'd be happy to drive."

"Oh, no," she said. "Let's take my car."

"Then follow me over to the police station. I'll drop my wheels there."

How had this happened? She was drawn to Sawyer like some cheap magnet to a refrigerator. He could see the attraction, yet he had some crazy ethical, moral or puritanical code—she wasn't sure which—that prevented him from acting on it.

So, however much she tried to avoid it, she'd be squirming in her seat for days, and he'd be determined to withstand it. To prevail.

It made her furious. With herself and with him. "I'll get my bag," she said. "While you're waiting, find a thermos. I think there's one in those cupboards. I'm gonna want coffee."

SAWYER PULLED INTO a truck stop shortly after seven. They'd beaten the rush-hour traffic, scooting out of the Chicagoland area before lots of commuters hit the road. It had been a straight shot north up I-94, and now they were headed west, just twenty minutes shy of Madison.

Liz hadn't said a word to him since they'd left his car at the station and he'd climbed into hers. Not even when he'd ask her if he could drive. She'd just looked at him and dropped the keys to her Toyota into his open hand. He'd pushed the seat back and tried to get comfortable. She'd sat on her side of the car, drank coffee, fiddled with the radio stations and generally ignored him.

He didn't care. A little dislike between him and Liz could go a long way. He hoped it went far enough that it kept him from wanting her, from taking her into his arms, from pulling her under his body.

He didn't think he'd be satisfied with less. He knew he didn't have a right to ask for more. He needed to keep his hands on the wheel and let her be pissed off at him. It was safer and ultimately easier and better for the both of them.

"I'm hungry," he said.

"Fine." She barely spared him a look before she turned her face to the window.

"We need gas, too."

"Fine," she repeated. She reached down between her feet, opened her purse and pulled out a twenty.

"I'll buy gas," Sawyer told her. "This is police business."

"Your boss knows you're going?"

"Of course. He thinks it's probably a wild-goose chase. But since Mirandez has had us chasing our tails for over a year, he's pulling out all the stops."

"When we find Mary, I'd appreciate it if you'd let me talk to her first. She'll be scared."

She had no idea she was playing into Lieutenant Fischer's hands. That was exactly what the man had hoped for. The lieutenant wanted Liz to draw Mary in, to get her to testify against Mirandez. Lord, he hated using Liz like this. "I'll do my best." Sawyer heard the stiffness in his voice. He ignored the quick look Liz shot in his direction and pulled the keys out of the ignition. "Let's go."

Sawyer took the lead, but no one even glanced up when they walked through the door. Not until Liz walked past the two men who were sitting in the middle booth drinking coffee. Sawyer heard the soft whistle first, then "Wouldn't mind having those wrapped around my waist."

Sawyer stopped in his tracks. He balled up his fist and turned.

# Chapter Eight

"Sawyer, please," she said. "Let it go."

It was the look in her eyes that stopped him. She didn't want a scene. Sawyer gave the men a look, and they had the good sense to take an interest in their eggs. He turned, walked another ten feet and slid into the empty booth at the end of the row. He faced the door. "They're stupid," he said.

"Agreed," she answered.

"You should wear pants," he lectured her. "No," he said, shaking his head. "That's not fair."

She waved a hand. "Nor practical. It's going to be a hundred degrees today." She picked up the plastic-covered listing of the day's specials.

"I imagine women get tired of men acting like idiots."

She sighed. Loudly. "Yes. Especially when they have dirty hair, food on their faces and bellies that hang over their pants."

It didn't take much for him to remember how he'd ogled those same legs last night. Yeah, his face and hair had been clean and his stomach still fairly flat, but that didn't make him much better than those creeps.

"How much farther?" she asked.

"We're twenty minutes east of Madison. Then it's another hour or so north to Wisconsin Dells. Our first stop is Clover Corners."

She shook her head, apparently not recognizing the name. "Why there?"

"Like I said earlier, we look everywhere. But there are a few places that seem more logical than others, so we start there."

"I'm not sure I understand the logic."

"I know Mirandez. He's a low-profile kind of guy. That's what has kept him alive so long."

"I thought you said he was twenty-six."

"You meet very few middle-aged gang leaders."

"I suppose. What kind of fishing would a low-profile type of guy do?"

"He'd look for a place where he could stay, eat and buy his bait without ever having to venture out. Especially because he probably can't go anywhere without dragging Mary with him. People notice pregnant women."

Liz nodded in agreement. "Last week when I went shopping with her, four people stopped to pat her stomach. Four complete strangers."

He didn't want to talk about Mary's pregnancy.

"It's like her stomach has become community property," Liz continued. "I told her she should get a sign for around her neck."

Despite himself, he wanted to know. "What would it say?"

"Something along the lines of Beware of Teeth. Then they wouldn't be able to sue her when she bit their hand."

There'd been a couple times that Mary had looked as if she wanted to bite him. Maybe a quick couple of nips out of his rear.

"But the really sick part is that I—"

"Two coffees here?" A waitress on her way past their booth stopped suddenly. She dropped a couple menus down on the corner of the table.

"Just water, please," Liz replied.

"Coffee would be fine," Sawyer said. Liz hadn't shared in the car. She'd been too busy being mad at him.

The waitress walked away. "What's the really sick part?" Sawyer asked.

Liz leaned forward. "Sometimes, I just can't help myself. I just have to touch their stomachs. I always thought that a pregnant woman's stomach would be soft, like a baby is soft. But it's this hard volleyball. It's so cool."

It had been cool. Cool and magical. His girlfriend had been thin. She hadn't actually showed for the better part of four months. And then one day, her flat little stomach had just popped out. And suddenly the baby had been real. He'd had no trouble at all suddenly visualizing what his son or daughter would look like, how he or she would run around the backyard at his parents' house, how he or she would hold his hand on the first day of school.

Even though he was just a kid himself, becoming a dad hadn't scared him.

He'd been too damn stupid to be scared.

He hadn't even considered that his child would be born weak, suffering, too small to take on the world.

He'd learned the hard way. Babies weren't tough at all.

The waitress came back with their drinks. "What can I get you this morning?"

"A bagel and cream cheese, please," Liz said.

"That's it?" Sawyer frowned at her.

She nodded.

Well, hell. He couldn't force her to eat. "Ham, eggs, hash-brown potatoes, and a side of biscuits and gravy," Sawyer said. The waitress wrote it down and left.

"Work up an appetite driving?" Liz asked.

Yeah, but not for food. But he wasn't going there. He'd managed to pull back last night. It had cost him. He'd spent most of the night mentally kicking his own butt. It hadn't helped that he knew he'd done the right thing. No, he'd been wound too tight, been too close to the edge. He'd wanted her badly.

But he couldn't sleep with Liz. Not with the possibility that he was going to have to arrest Mary. He knew that once he slept with Liz, once he let her into his soul, he'd be hard-pressed to be objective about Mary. And he couldn't afford to let up on the pursuit of Mirandez now. Not when they were so close.

"You may be sorry," he said. "We're not stopping again until lunch."

"It'll be okay. If I get hungry, I'll gnaw off a couple fingers."

"Mine or yours?" The minute he said it, he was sorry. He didn't need to be thinking about her mouth on any part of his body. "Just remember," he said, working hard to keep his voice from cracking, "the per diem reimbursement rate is $50 a person per day. They actually expect us to eat."

"Last of the big spenders, huh?"

"Big spender? The city? No. They barely buy us office supplies."

She put her elbows on the table and rested her chin on her hands. "Did you always want to be a cop, Sawyer? Was that your dream?"

His dream had been to raise his child. "No."

"How did you end up wearing a badge?"

It had seemed like the only thing to do. "I didn't go on to college right out of high school. I worked for a while." He'd worked like a dog when he'd found out Terrie was pregnant. He'd been determined to provide for her and his child. It was afterward, when he faced the truth that Terrie had continued to use drugs during the pregnancy, that he thought he'd worked too much. He'd been so focused on providing for his child that he'd neglected to protect him.

"But then…things happened, and I decided I wasn't going to get anywhere without an education. I started at the junior college and then went on for a bachelor's degree. I've been a cop for fifteen years. I don't know how to do much else."

"You haven't been in Chicago for fifteen years."

"How do you know?"

She looked over both shoulders and leaned forward in the booth. "Like Mary said," she whispered, "you talk funny."

"I do not. You people in the north talk funny."

"I wouldn't say that too loudly. A body can go missing in the woods for a long time before somebody stumbles upon it."

"Duly noted."

"Why Chicago?"

"Why not?" He took a drink of coffee. That was probably all he needed to say, but suddenly he wanted to tell her more. "My father died two years ago. My mom had passed the year before. With both of them gone, there was no reason to stay in Baton Rouge."

"Aha. Baton Rouge. I had guessed New Orleans."

"I spent some time there."

She settled back in her booth. "Drinking Hurricanes at Pat O'Brien's? Eating beignets at Café du Monde? Brunch at the Court of Two Sisters?"

He'd been working undercover, mostly setting up drug buys with the underbelly of society. "Sounds like you know the place."

"I did an internship there when I was working on my doctorate. I loved everything about it. The food especially. After I left, I dreamed of gumbo."

"I can do a crawfish boil better than most."

She sighed. "Don't tease me. You don't really know how to cook, do you?"

His mother had believed that cooking was everybody's

work. In the South, family meant food. Hell, maybe when this was all over, he'd have Liz over for dinner.

Maybe they'd eat in bed. He'd feed her shrimp creole and drizzle the sauce across her naked body.

Lord help him. He reached for his water and knocked his silverware on the floor.

She scooted out of the booth and reached over to the next table to grab him a fresh set. He saw the smooth, tanned skin of her back when her shirt pulled up.

He did a quick look to make sure the two goons in the middle booth weren't copping a look.

Nope. It was just him.

"No other family there?" she asked.

"What?" He shook his head, trying to clear it.

She slid the silverware toward him. "Do you have other family in Baton Rouge?"

He'd brought Jake with him. That had taken some doing, but there'd been no other option. "No." She was getting too close. He needed to change the subject.

"How about you?" he asked. "Did you always want to be a social worker at OCM?"

"No, I worked in private practice for several years. Sort of chasing the American dream. You know, a fancy house, a new car, trips to Europe, three-hundred-dollar suits."

He knew that much. He wanted to know why she'd left it all behind. "Doesn't sound all that bad."

"It's not bad. Just not enough."

He let her words hang. When she didn't continue, he jumped in, not wanting the conversation to die. "Just decided you'd had enough of living in the lap of luxury?"

She smiled, a sad sort of half smile. "You got it. Decided I couldn't take any more caviar and champagne."

He thought about pushing. Over the course of his career, he'd persuaded street-smart drug dealers, high-priced hookers and numbers-running bookies to talk. Some had been easier than others. But he rarely failed.

But he didn't want to pry or coerce Liz into offering up information. Maybe it was as simple as she made it sound. Maybe she just got tired of the fast lane. If so, no doubt it would lure her back, sooner or later. She'd get tired of slugging her way through the day at OCM, the hours filled with fights with belligerent teens.

If she didn't want to talk, okay with him. He didn't care what had driven her to OCM.

Right. He wanted to know. Wanted to know everything about her. Might have asked, too, if the waitress hadn't picked that moment to slam down their breakfasts in front of them. He picked up his fork, dug into his eggs, grateful for the diversion.

They didn't speak again until they were both finished eating. "I've got a picture of Mirandez in the car," Sawyer said. "It's a good shot, shows his face really well. When we get to each place, you can go into the office and show Mary's picture as well as Mirandez's."

"And if they haven't seen them?"

"We move on. But leave a card. Put my cell-phone number on the back." He reached out, tore off a corner of the paper place mat and wrote down the number. "Oh, by the way—" he tried for nonchalant "—when I was doing my internet searches, I got us a place to stay."

Liz was glad she had finished breakfast. Otherwise, she might have choked on her bagel. He made it sound so married-like. As if they were on vacation and he'd taken care of the reservations: *Hey, honey. We're going to the Days Inn.*

Problem was, they weren't married and this was no vacation.

"Where?" she managed to ask.

"Lake Weston. It's on the west side of The Dells. It's centrally located to the search. There weren't a lot of vacancies. I guess this is prime vacation season. Everybody's here with their kids, a last fling before school starts."

*Please, Liz, let me come before school starts.* Jenny had called her at work. It had been a crazy summer for Liz. One of the other partners had been gone from work for months. He'd had a heart attack, and Liz had worried that the rest of the staff would have one, too, if they kept up the pace. Everyone was working six days a week, twelve hours a day. But still, when Jenny had called, she'd agreed to let her come. Jenny, at sixteen, loved the city. Its diversity, its energy, its passion for music and art.

Liz had managed to squeeze out time to shop, to go out to eat and even for a concert at Grant Park. Four days after she'd arrived, Liz had kissed Jenny goodbye and sent her home on the train. Three months later, Jenny had been dead.

"What are you thinking about?" Sawyer asked. "You look like you're a million miles away."

Liz debated whether she should tell him. Even after three years, it was difficult to talk about Jenny and the hole that her death had made.

"My little sister used to visit me in the summers. She told me it was better than a weekend at Six Flags."

Sawyer laughed. "Not bad. You edged out an amusement park. How old was she?"

"Sixteen." She'd always be sixteen in Liz's mind.

"Wow. A lot younger than you. Second marriage for one of your parents?"

"No. Just a bonus baby. I was thirteen when she was born."

"She in college now?" Sawyer asked.

"No." Liz gripped the edge of the Formica-topped table. "She's... Jenny's dead."

She could see his chest rise and fall with a deep breath. "I'm sorry," he said. "What happened?"

"She killed herself. In the bathroom of my parents' house. She bled to death in the bathtub."

He didn't know what to say. "Did she leave a note?"

"No. I'm not sure if that makes it more or less horrible."

"Do you have any idea why?"

"She was eight weeks pregnant. According to her best friend, the father of the baby had taken back his ring just two days before."

Sawyer shook his head. "I'm sorry."

He was sorry, and she hadn't even told him the worst part. The part that had almost destroyed her until she'd found OCM.

"I guess I understand why it's so important for you to help Mary."

He had no idea. "Let's just say I don't want another girl to fall through the cracks." It was the same thing she'd told Jamison. There wasn't really a better way to sum it up.

"Right." Sawyer folded up his paper napkin. "You know," he said, his voice hesitant, "Mary might be hiding in one of those cracks. She and Mirandez. She had the chance to point the finger at him. But she wouldn't."

"I don't know why," Liz said. "Maybe she's afraid of him?"

"If she's smart, she is. If she's lying about him being the father, maybe she's trying to get him to marry her? Maybe he's a meal ticket?"

It was possible. She might see it as a better alternative than working her whole life. "When we find them, I'll ask her."

Sawyer slid out of the booth. "I hope like hell you get the chance."

## Chapter Nine

At each place, it was the same. Liz showed Mary's picture first, then Mirandez's. Then she'd tell the story. She'd been working in Europe for the past year and had missed her sister's wedding. Having just returned, she hoped to surprise the bride and groom.

Everyone had looked at the pictures, shaken their heads, taken her card and agreed to call her if the couple checked in. Sawyer had concocted the story, hoping that people's inherent love of a good surprise would keep any clerk from telling Mary and Mirandez that someone had asked about them. And if someone did have loose lips, perhaps Mirandez wouldn't be too nervous if he thought only Liz had followed Mary.

They'd stopped at ten places before noon. "How's that bagel holding up?" Sawyer asked.

"We can stop if you're hungry," she said.

"You don't eat lunch?"

She waved a hand. "Sure I do."

"Uh-huh. What did you have for lunch yesterday?"

Liz chewed on her lip. "Chips and a can of pop."

"The day before?"

"Oh, for goodness' sake. I had…chips and a pop."

He leaned across the seat and inspected her. "You don't *look* like you've got scurvy," he said.

She let out a huff of air. "I take a multivitamin every day. Oh, damn." She smacked herself on the forehead. "I think I forgot my vitamins."

Sawyer shook his head. Ten minutes later, he turned the car into a gas station. Half the building was a convenience store. "I'll get us some lunch." He opened his door. "So, what kind of chips do you like?"

She smiled. "You're not going to try to reform me?"

"I'm smarter than that. Do you want to come in?"

"No. I need to call Jamison. I left a message on his machine early this morning. That was before I knew we would be traveling together."

"What's he going to think about that?"

"He'll be thrilled. He'll think I'm safer."

"You like Jamison, don't you?"

"He's a great boss. He trusts all of us. He knows we work hard, and he's really loyal in return. He treats us more like good friends than employees."

"He and Fraypish are friends, right?"

"For over twenty years. Jamison really respects Howard's legal judgment." Liz pulled out her cell phone and started dialing. "And he works at the right price, too."

Sawyer slammed the door shut. He didn't really care about what Jamison thought about Fraypish. He wanted to know what Liz thought about the man.

Why? He pushed open the door of the convenience store. Why did it matter? He and Liz had shared a couple kisses. Okay, a couple of really hot kisses that had made his knees weak, but still, it meant nothing. They would hopefully find Mary safe. She'd turn on Mirandez, and months from now, if he and Liz happened to run into each other at the grocery store, they'd nod politely and go their separate ways.

He grabbed an extralarge bag of potato chips. What did he care if she got fat and had bad skin?

He walked over to the counter and picked out two ham-and-cheese sandwiches. He stuck two cans of pop in the crook of his arm. A young woman at the cash register stopped filing her nails so that she could ring him up.

"Will that be all?" he asked.

"You don't happen to stock multivitamins?"

She shook her head.

"Got any fresh fruit?"

She pointed to the back of the store. "Bananas. Fifty cents apiece."

"I'll take six." When he got to the car, Liz was just snapping shut her cell phone. He dropped the bag into her lap. She reached inside and pulled out the chips.

"A big bag," she said, looking pleased. She pulled out the soda. "Thank you very much," she said. She handed him the bag, but he didn't take it.

"There's something else for you," he said.

She peered inside the plastic bag. A smile, so genuine that it reached her pretty green eyes, lit up her face. "You bought me bananas."

You'd have thought it was expensive perfume or something that sparkled. He opened his own soda and took a big drink. Liz Mayfield made a man thirsty. "I can probably find us a picnic table somewhere," he said.

She shook her head and ripped open her bag of chips. "Let's just keep going."

They stopped at another eleven places before Sawyer finally pulled into the parking lot of Lake Weston. It was after seven, they hadn't had dinner and Liz looked exhausted. She had dutifully gotten out at each stop, given her spiel and returned to the car, looking more and more discouraged.

"Look, here's our place. I think we should call it a night," Sawyer said. "Neither of us got much sleep last night. Let's get checked in, I'll find us some food, and you can crash."

"No."

It was the first word she'd said in two hours.

"What?"

"No. We have to keep going. Let's just grab a sandwich. We can probably hit three or four more places tonight."

"Liz, be reasonable. It'll be dark in another hour. We'll get a fresh start in the morning."

Liz picked the map up and spread it across her lap. "Look, there're two places just ten miles or so up the road. We're wasting time."

He was going to have to strap her down. But he didn't think he had the energy.

He shook his head. "We have to get checked in. They close the office at eight. We need to get a key to our cabin."

"Cabin?" she repeated.

"I got a *two*-bedroom cabin. It was all they had. I hope you don't mind sharing a bath."

"Oh. No, of course not. It sounds great. I mean, it sounds like it will suit our needs. Enough space, you know."

She was blushing. He didn't get it. Had she really thought he'd only book one room? Maybe in his wildest dreams. "You're going to have to register. It's in your name. If Mirandez happened to track you back here, I didn't want there to be any record of me. Only problem is, you'll have to put it on your credit card. The department will reimburse you."

"That's fine." She opened her car door. "I'll get us registered. And then we're going to the next two on the map. Their offices might close around eight, too. We'll need to hurry."

The woman was a workhorse. "Fine. We'll go to those two. But then we're done. And I'm picking the restaurant. Get prepared because there may not be chips on the menu."

IT WAS ALMOST NINE O'CLOCK when Sawyer ordered steaks for both of them. He'd found a supper club alongside the highway. The parking lot had been full, and he'd taken that as an endorsement.

The lighting was a little too dim, the music a little too loud. But the chairs were soft, and the cold beer he held in his hand tasted really good.

He thought Liz might fall asleep in her chair. Her eyes were half-closed. She looked pale, tired and defenseless. And it made him want to slay dragons for her.

If—or when, he corrected himself, trying to think a bit more positively—he found Mary, he would kick her butt for making this woman worry. For making the two of them traipse across the country in a hot car that didn't have a working air conditioner.

He wished he'd learned that little piece of information earlier. Like before he'd left his own car at the station and decided to take a road trip in the Toastermobile. He'd turned the knob just after breakfast this morning, when the temperature had already hit the low nineties, and hot air had blown in his face. He'd looked at Liz, and she'd shrugged her shoulders and looked the happiest she had all morning.

Looking back, it had been an omen of how the day would go. One big bust.

But through it all, Liz had moved forward without complaint. He'd driven, and she'd read the map, directing him from place to place. Her instructions had been clear and succinct. At each stop, she'd gotten out and flashed her pictures. She hadn't whined or complained. Hell, she could probably slay her own dragons. She was tough enough.

"We'll go north tomorrow," he said. He picked up a roll, buttered it and held it out to her. She shook her head no. He kept his hand extended and raised one eyebrow.

"I'm too tired to fight," she said, and she grabbed it out of his hand.

He waited until she took a dainty little bite before continuing, "Thank you. You don't eat enough."

"I ate a banana."

"So you did. Maybe that will be enough to keep you from falling down."

"If it's not, just prop me up and drive to the next place."

He laughed until he realized she was half-serious. "You're not going to give up, are you?"

"No. I can't. I won't."

"What happens if we don't find Mary?"

"We will. If we look hard enough, we will."

God, he hoped he didn't have to disappoint her. "Probably no need to start so early tomorrow. Maybe you could catch up on your rest."

"I'm not tired."

No, of course not. "Yeah, well, I am."

She blinked twice. "No, you're not." She shook her head at him. "You think by saying that you're tired that I'll implicitly understand that it's okay if I'm tired."

Why did she have to be a psychologist? Why couldn't she have been an accountant or an engineer?

"Did it work?" he asked.

"No. I'm fine. Don't worry about me."

"Okay. But could you at least drink your water? Just being in the car today was enough to dehydrate a person."

"Where did you get your medical degree?"

He didn't take offense. She'd smiled at him. The first one of those he'd seen in a couple of hours.

"Off the street of hard knocks. It's a fast-track program. You do your internship at a homeless shelter and your residency in the emergency room at Melliertz Hospital. They don't have metal screeners there for nothing."

"I'll bet you've seen a lot of violence, huh?"

She leaned her head back against the chair. The flickering

light from the cheesy candle on the table danced across the long lines of her graceful neck. She was a beautiful woman.

"I'll bet you've *heard* about a lot of violence," he replied. "I wonder what's worse. Seeing it or hearing about it."

A cloud of sadness drifted across her face. "I think seeing it," she said. "When you hear about it, you can't imagine how horrific it really is. Your mind just won't let you go there."

He had a bad feeling about this. He figured there was only one way to ask the question. "You're the one who found your sister?"

"Yes."

"What happened?" He braced himself, having investigated a few of those types of calls over the years. It was gruesome, ugly work.

"I tried her on the telephone but didn't get an answer. After a couple of hours, I drove out to my parents' house. They were gone for the weekend. She'd been dead for several hours when I found her."

He knew exactly what it had looked and smelled like. He hoped like hell that they didn't run into something similar with Mary. That Mirandez hadn't spirited the girl away just so he could kill her and dump her body up in the boondocks. "I'm sorry," he said, thinking it sounded a bit inadequate.

"I am, too," she said, her voice trembling just a little. "But thank you. It's still hard for me to talk about it. For some reason, you made it easier."

It wasn't a dragon but close. A sense of satisfaction, a sense of peace, filled him.

The waiter arrived at their table, his arms laden with heavy serving platters. He set two sizzling steaks down in front of them with sides of baked potato and fresh green beans.

Sawyer picked up his fork. "Bon appétit," he said. In return, she smiled and picked up her own utensils.

Twenty minutes later, the dishes had all been cleared away. Sawyer sipped a cup of steaming-hot coffee and watched Liz. She'd done better with dinner than she had with breakfast or lunch. She'd managed to eat at least half the steak and most of the potato. "Let's get out of here," he said when he saw her head jerk back. She was literally falling asleep sitting up. Within a couple of minutes, he'd settled the bill and walked her out of the restaurant. He kept his hand firmly planted underneath her elbow. It felt so right that he refused to think about all the reasons it was wrong.

A ten-minute drive got them back to the cabin. "Let me check it out," Sawyer ordered. He opened the compartment between the two seats and pulled out the gun that she'd seen him shove inside earlier. When he got out, he quickly walked to the cabin door, the barrel of the gun pointed upward. He twisted the doorknob, evidently found it locked, because she watched as he unlocked the heavy door with the real key the office had given them. Then in one fluid motion, he swung his body inside. Within seconds he was back, motioning for her to get out of the car. "Looks okay," he said. He waited for her to get inside, then pulled the door shut behind them, turned the lock and looked with some disgust at the flimsy chain before hooking it.

"What were you expecting?" she asked.

"I didn't know. A good cop just expects something."

Sawyer Montgomery was a very good cop. She stood somewhat awkwardly by the door. The cabin wasn't big but comfortable enough. The small sitting area had two chairs, a lamp table and a stone fireplace. A sign posted on the fireplace warned against actually using it. To the right, pushed up against the wall, was a double bed. To the left, two doors. She walked across the scarred but clean wooden floor and peeked into the first one.

Okay. Small but neat. The bath had a white tile floor and

pale blue walls. Above the shower stall was a small, high window with a faded yellow shade.

She moved on to the second door. Reaching inside the door, she found the light switch. A single bed with a dark green bedspread and small dresser almost filled the space. The switch controlled the floor lamp next to the bed. Its dim light barely reached the corners of the room.

"It's kind of a two-bedroom," Sawyer said, standing directly behind her.

"It's fine," Liz said. "Which bed do you want?" she asked.

Sawyer edged past her and in four steps walked across the small room. He lifted the inexpensive white plastic blinds and inspected the windows. They were double-paned and locked from the inside.

"I'll take the one in the other room."

The room with the door that had the no-real-protection lock. Yes, Sawyer Montgomery was a good cop. Even though she was more than a hundred miles from home, physically exhausted and in a cabin with a man she'd only known for a couple days, she felt safe.

"If you hear anything, and I mean anything," he continued, "you come get me. I'm a light sleeper."

Thinking about him sleeping just twenty feet away from her did funny things to her insides. "I'm sure it'll be fine," she said.

"Just don't hesitate," he said. "Why don't you use the bathroom first? I've got to make a couple calls and check messages." He pulled one of the chairs closer to the lamp table. Liz grabbed her bag by the door and took it into the bathroom with her.

Sawyer waited until he heard the shower running before dialing Robert's cell phone. When it rang four times, Sawyer got worried that Robert had some hot date. He breathed a sigh of relief when it was answered on the seventh ring.

"Why, it's Fisherman Sawyer," Robert said.

There were times when caller ID was inconvenient. "I figured the lieutenant would fill you in."

"Oh, yeah. Where are you?"

"Halfway between Madison and Hell."

Now it was Robert's turn to laugh. "I've been there. Lots of potholes and greasy-spoon restaurants. Is our little piranha biting?"

"No. I didn't really expect him to. I think I'm on a wild-goose chase."

"How's Liz?"

*Wonderful. Gorgeous. Strong.* "Fine. A little tired. It's been a long day."

"You planning on letting her get any sleep tonight?"

Sawyer could hear the tease in his partner's voice. It didn't matter. *Liz* and *bed* in the same sentence wasn't funny. "None of your business," he said.

"She's gotten to you, hasn't she?" Robert asked, his voice more serious than usual.

"She's…interesting."

"Six-legged spiders are interesting."

"Them, too. Look, I better go."

"Well, before you do, you might want to know this. Fluentes thinks Mirandez has a sister somewhere in Wisconsin."

"What? I don't think that's possible." Sawyer ran his hands through his hair. "I've never seen any mention of siblings. Not anywhere."

"Well, rumor has it he's got a much older sister. Hardly anybody has ever seen her, but she evidently came home for their old man's funeral a few years ago."

A sister? Was it possible that Mirandez had sought refuge with his family?

"Fluentes have a name?" Sawyer asked. "Was the sister married?"

"I told you everything I know."

"Okay. Thanks." Sawyer hung up just as Liz came out of the bathroom. She had on clean shorts and a T-shirt. She gave him a quick wave and slipped into the bedroom, closing the door behind her.

Liz closed the door and flipped the light switch off. In two steps, she reached the bed. She pulled the bedspread and thin blanket back all the way, leaving them at the end of the bed. She slipped under the cool sheet and hoped for sleep.

She rubbed her elbow. In the shower, she'd almost scrubbed it raw, in some silly hope that she could erase the feel of Sawyer's hand as he'd cupped her elbow and guided her across the parking lot. She could still feel his heat, his strength, his goodness.

It had been a long time since a man had taken care of her. The last serious relationship she'd had, she'd taken care of the man. Not in the physical sense certainly but in almost every other way.

She'd been a twenty-five-year-old virgin when she'd met Ted. Theodore Rainey. They'd dated for two years before he'd asked her to marry him. She'd accepted both his engagement ring and the invitation to sleep in his bed. A year later, after three wedding dates had come and gone, canceled due to Ted's work schedule, it had seemed as if they'd never manage to get married.

She knew she should have looked beyond his feeble excuses and tried to understand the real reason he avoided marriage. She supposed that was why psychologists never treated themselves. They had no objectivity. Had one of her patients described the relationship that Liz had with Ted, Liz would have advised her to get out of it.

In the end, they'd parted almost amicably. By that time, the sex was infrequent, generally hurried and rarely fulfilling. It had been a relief not to have to pretend anymore.

Liz pulled the sheet up another couple of inches, snuggling into the cool bed. As she drifted off to sleep, she thought about the lucky woman who shared Sawyer's bed, knowing in her heart that that woman wouldn't spend much time pretending.

## Chapter Ten

Liz woke up when she heard the shower turn on. The walls of the cabin were perhaps not paper-thin but pretty darn close. She heard a thud and a soft curse. Sounded as if Sawyer was having a little trouble with the narrow stall.

She slipped out of bed, walked over to the window and peeked through the slats of the blinds. Looked like a pretty day. Bright sunshine with just a few puffy clouds. Maybe it would be a few degrees cooler than the day before. It had been a real scorcher. She'd known her air-conditioning didn't work, but in some juvenile way, it had been her way of one-upping Sawyer. He'd been so high-handed about coming with her that she figured she owed him one.

But then later, when he remained in the hot car while she at least got a few breaks going into the mostly air-conditioned offices, and he didn't complain even once, she began to feel bad. When he'd bought her bananas, she'd felt very stupid and very petty. She intended to start this day off better. She'd seen the sign in the office area last night that promoted the free continental breakfast for guests. She could go grab a couple cups of coffee, maybe some chocolate doughnuts if she got really lucky and be back before Sawyer got out of the shower.

She slipped her feet into sandals and grabbed her purse off the old dresser. When she opened the front door, she sucked in a deep breath, cherishing the still-cool early-morning air. It was probably not much past seven. When she got to the office, she had to wait a few minutes while a young family, a man, woman and three small children, worked their way past the rolls and bagels, assorted juices and blessed coffee.

No chocolate doughnuts but there was a close second—pecan rolls. She put two on a plate and then grabbed a bagel and cream cheese for good measure. Sawyer ate a lot. She poured two cups of coffee and balanced them in one hand, grateful for the summer she'd spent waiting tables. When she got to the door, the young man who'd gotten his family settled around the one lone table got up and opened it for her.

Liz strolled across the parking lot, loving the smell of the hot coffee. Unable to resist, she stopped, took a small sip from one of the cups, burned her tongue just a bit and swallowed with gusto. Little topped that first taste of coffee in the morning.

When she got outside the cabin door, she carefully set both coffees and the plate of pastries down on the sidewalk. She used her key to open the door. Then she bent down, picked up her cache and pushed the door open the rest of the way with her foot. She went inside and turned to shut the door. And then she almost dropped her precious brew.

Sawyer, wearing nothing but a pair of unsnapped jeans, had a gun pointed at her chest.

"What the hell do you think you're doing?" he asked.

What was *she* doing? "Are you going to shoot me?"

"Don't ever do that again," he instructed, ignoring her question.

"Do what?" She threw his words back at him. Darn, he had some nerve. He'd scared ten years off her, and he acted as if *he'd* been wronged. Before she dropped them, she put the coffees and the pastry plate on the table.

He closed the gap between them, never taking his dark

brown eyes off her face. He carefully placed his gun next
to the plate. "Well, for starters," he said, his words clipped
short, his accent more pronounced, "don't ever leave without telling me where you're going."

He acted as if she'd been gone for three days. "Sawyer,
you're being ridiculous. I walked across the parking lot."

He grabbed both of her arms. "Listen to me. You don't
open a door, you don't answer a phone, you don't—"

She tried to pull away, but his hold was firm. "I'm not
your prisoner. You're not responsible for me."

He was close enough that she could see the muscle in his
jaw jerk. "I am. Make no mistake about that. You do what
I tell you to do when I tell you to do it. This is police business, and I'm in charge."

"I thought you might appreciate coffee. If I'd known that
I might get shot for it, I wouldn't have bothered."

He stood close enough that she could smell him. The
clean, edgy scent of an angry man. His bare chest loomed
close enough that all she had to do was reach out and she
would be touching his naked skin. She let her eyes drift down
across his chest, following the line of hair as it tapered down
into the open V of his unbuttoned jeans.

Oh, my.

She flicked her eyes up. His breath was shallow, drawn
through just slightly open lips. His eyes seemed even darker.

And then he closed the distance between them and pulled
her body up next to his, fitting her curves into his strength.
He pushed his hips against hers, confirming what her eyes
had discovered.

He was hard.

"This is crazy," she said. "We can't—"

"Just shut up," he murmured, and then he bent his head
and kissed her. As wild as his eyes had been, she expected
the kiss to be hard, brutal. But it wasn't. His lips were warm

and soft, and he tasted like mint. She opened her mouth, and he angled his head, bringing them closer until she no longer knew where he stopped and she began. He rocked against her, and she thought she might split apart because the pleasure was so intense.

She moved her hands across his broad back, then lower, dipping her fingertips just inside the waistband of his jeans. She lightly scraped her nails across his bare, hot skin, and when he groaned, she felt the power of being a woman. It soared through her, heating her.

He moved his own hands, pushing them up inside her loose shirt. When all he encountered was bare skin, his big body literally shuddered. She pushed her hands deeper into his jeans, under the cotton material of his briefs, cupping each bare cheek. He pulled his mouth away from hers. "You're driving me crazy."

That made her braver, made her feel even more powerful. She found his lips again and kissed him hard. And she arched against his body, greedy with her need to touch him everywhere. "I want you to—"

The shrill ring of a cell phone cut her off. Sawyer pulled away from her and reached across the table to check his phone.

"It's mine," Liz managed. "It's in my purse."

She grabbed the still-ringing phone. Remembering his orders that she couldn't answer the phone without his permission, she looked at him. The phone rang two more times before he nodded. Liz hurriedly pushed a button. "Hello," she said.

"Liz, you were supposed to call me yesterday."

Howard Fraypish. She'd forgotten all about him. "I'm sorry, Howard. I had a few things to take care of."

She covered the mouthpiece with her hand and whispered to Sawyer, "I'll be just a minute. It's Howard."

Sawyer raised an eyebrow.

"We're working on a placement."

"Sure. Whatever." He walked across the room. She watched him pull a T-shirt out of his bag. He pulled it on in one smooth motion.

"...and I need to make sure that Melissa hasn't changed her mind. The Partridges don't want to be disappointed."

She'd totally missed the first part when she'd been ogling Sawyer's bare chest. "No, Howard. I spoke with her just a couple days ago. She's definitely giving the baby up for adoption. I don't think she's going to change her mind. She should deliver by the end of next week. And then two weeks after that, she leaves for college."

"Call me the minute she delivers."

"I will, but don't worry. She knows you're handling the legal work. I told you that I'd told her to call you directly if she can't reach me."

"Oh, yeah."

He sounded so distracted. "Is something wrong, Howard?"

"What could be wrong? I'm just busy. Really busy. I've got to go. Goodbye, Liz."

Liz snapped her phone shut. Sawyer stood next to the table, drinking one of the cups of coffee.

"You want the bagel?" he asked.

So, he wanted to pretend that the past ten minutes hadn't happened. That they hadn't argued, that they hadn't practically swallowed each other up. No, she wouldn't let him do it. Even if it meant that she had to admit that she'd come close to begging him to take her to bed.

"What's going on here, Sawyer?"

He stared at her for a long minute. "When I got out of the shower and I couldn't find you, I got worried. It was less than a week ago that somebody made a threat to your life.

Now, I know you think that it was just some kid but maybe not. Even if it was, we're on this crazy chase after Mirandez. I know you don't understand how dangerous he is. But if you're right that he and Mary are here and he finds out that you're looking for him, there's no telling what he might do. The man has no conscience. He kills people like the rest of us kill bugs."

Well, okay. "I'm sorry. I should have said something before I went for coffee."

He shrugged his shoulders. "Just forget it."

Forget that he'd kissed her? Was it that easy for him? "We got a little carried away here," she reminded him.

He nodded. "You're right. I'm attracted to you, Liz. But to act upon it would be absolutely wrong on my part. Whether you like it or not, I am responsible for this operation. And that includes you."

"I'm a big girl, Sawyer. I take responsibility for my own actions."

"And I take responsibility for mine."

He didn't sound too happy about it. "Sawyer, I don't understand why we can't—"

"Because I can't lose focus. My job is to find Mirandez. And to arrest him, with solid enough evidence that the guys in suits have no trouble getting a conviction."

"I'm trying to help you."

"I appreciate that. But what happens when Mary is part of that evidence? What happens if I have to arrest her, too? I can't let you and how you feel about Mary keep me from doing my job."

"I wouldn't ask you to do that," she said, not understanding why he couldn't see that. She'd never put him in that position.

"You wouldn't have to," he said, his voice soft.

IF POSSIBLE, LIZ THOUGHT the temperature had shot even higher than the day before. By ten o'clock, after just a couple hours in the car, they both looked a little wilted. They'd already been to four smaller campgrounds. One hadn't even had an office, so they'd had to be content with just driving through the camping area, looking at the various campsites. At the other three, the response had been virtually the same.

"Nope. They don't look familiar. But then again, we get a lot of people passing through. It would be pretty hard to remember everybody. Sure, you can check back. We're here from sunup to sundown most days."

Good old-fashioned Wisconsin charm. Liz wondered why she felt compelled to wring the next person's neck. Between the heat outside, the worry about Mary and the sexual tension radiating off Sawyer, she thought murder looked like a fairly good alternative.

He hadn't touched her again. Hadn't really said more than ten words to her. But each time she got out of the car and walked into one of the campground offices or when she walked back, she knew, just knew, that he watched her every step of the way. And while it seemed a little crazy, she thought she saw a hunger in his eyes. But then she'd get in the car and he'd be all business, all silent business, and she decided she had a case of wishful thinking and wicked thoughts.

She wanted Sawyer. She wanted to kiss him. After all, the man had the kind of lips that you could kiss for about three straight weeks without coming up for air. And then she wanted him naked.

She'd only ever slept with one man. But now all she could think about was getting it on with a man she'd known for less than a week.

It made her feel disloyal to Mary. Mary had to be the priority. And Liz knew what happened when priorities got mixed up. She couldn't bear for that to happen again. Mary deserved more. Liz respected Sawyer's ability to stay on task. She felt slimy that her focus had slipped momentarily. It had been jarred by the incredible warmth of his body pressed up against hers.

But thankfully, Sawyer had pulled back in time. He'd done the right thing. So, she needed to stop being mad at him.

"How much farther north?" she asked.

Sawyer risked a quick look at her. He'd told himself he might get through the day if he just didn't have to look at her. Didn't have to see her pretty green eyes with the dark eyelashes that had literally fluttered down across her cheeks when he'd kissed her. Or her pink lips, the bottom one fuller than the top, that literally trembled when he'd brushed his hands across her breast.

She'd gathered her long hair up, twisted it in that way that only women knew how to do and clipped it on top of her head. In deference to the heat, she had on a white sleeveless one-piece cotton dress, the kind of shapeless thing that seemed so popular these days.

Not that the dress did him much good. He could still remember what every one of her curves felt like. Hell, the woman even had curvy feet. She had white sandals on that showed off her red-painted toes and the delicate arch of her small foot.

He put his eyes back on the road. Safer by a long shot. "I thought we'd go about thirty miles. Then we'll need to cross over and come down the other side. If we don't get it all done today, we'll have to come back tomorrow."

"Then what?"

"Tomorrow we'll go west toward Route 39. That's one of the main roads. Lots of tourists head up this way. There're a couple large lodges and camping areas."

"This is kind of like looking for a needle in a haystack, isn't it? I guess I didn't fully appreciate how difficult it might be."

"You want to turn back? You could be in your apartment by midafternoon."

"No. Absolutely not. I'm not giving up."

He hadn't expected any different. Liz seemed almost driven to help Mary.

"You must care a great deal about Mary," he said.

"I know it may be hard to understand. She's not all that easy to be around. She's at the stage of her life where she's very inner focused. Her needs, her wants, her pleasures take priority."

"Sounds like most teenagers."

"True." Liz smiled and he felt better. Lord, she was sunshine, all wrapped up into a nice portable package.

"Thankfully, most people grow out of it," she said. "Some never do. Some can't ever love another more than they love themselves."

It was the opening he'd waited for. He just didn't know if he had the courage to ask the question. "Sounds like you're speaking from experience?"

"Years of study."

Right. *Be bold or go home.* That was what the bumper sticker said that Robert had tacked up on his computer a couple years ago. "How's Howard feel about your leaving town with me?"

"Howard?" She looked genuinely puzzled. "How would he know?"

"He doesn't know you're with me? I thought that's why he called."

"He called about an adoption that he's working on."

"I figured that was just a pretense. I thought Jamison probably called him, and Fraypish decided it might be in his best interests to remind you not to forget him. I'm surprised he didn't demand that you come home. I know if you were dating me, you wouldn't be spending the night in a cabin with another man."

"Dating you?"

Now she looked a little green. Clearly the idea didn't have a lot of appeal. "Never mind," Sawyer mumbled. He sucked at bold.

"I'm not dating Howard."

"You two looked pretty friendly at the dance."

"We were dancing. It's hard to look like strangers when you're doing that. Howard wanted to take a date. I didn't have one. So, when he asked, I said yes. We met there. He didn't even pick me up."

"Hard to believe that you wouldn't have a date." *Lame. Lame. He was so lame.*

She chuckled. "There are worse things."

"Agreed. Still, seems like you'd have them lined up outside your door." He kept his eyes on the road, too scared to look at her and say the words.

She didn't say anything for a minute. He wondered if he'd offended her. He risked a quick look over.

"I almost got married a few years back," she said so matter-of-factly that he almost missed it. A hundred pounds, like barbells falling from a rack, seemed to land square on his lungs, making it hard to breathe.

"Married?" He managed to spit the word out.

"Someone that I used to work with," she said. "He's a nice enough guy. We just didn't want the same things."

He could imagine what the guy wanted from her. What every man, including him, would want. "What did you want?"

"Marriage. I suppose children."

She should have that. "Sounds reasonable," he managed

to say. Not for him, but then again, they weren't talking about him.

"Have you ever been married, Sawyer?"

"No."

"Come close?"

"Once."

"What happened?"

He wanted to tell her. Wanted to tell her about the whole stupid mess. But then she'd know he was a failure. That he hadn't been able to protect his son. That he hadn't been smart enough or brave enough. And then he'd see the pity in her eyes, the same pity he'd seen in the nurses' eyes, the doctors' eyes, the hospital chaplain's eyes. He couldn't stand that.

"We were both young," he said. "It probably wouldn't have worked out."

"Do you ever see her? Run into her at class reunions?"

"She's dead."

"Oh. I'm sorry."

"Yeah. Me, too." He meant that. He'd hated her. Hated her for what she'd done to his son. But even so, when he'd heard that she'd died of a drug overdose, just a couple years later, he'd mourned her loss. Another tragedy caused by drugs. And by the people like Mirandez who bankrolled the drugs into the country and then built a distribution system, mostly of kids, that rivaled those found at blue-chip companies.

"You must have loved her very much," Liz said.

He knew what she was thinking. She thought he was still in love with his dead girlfriend. He really wished it was as simple as that. "Sure," he said, choosing to let her continue down that path.

"Don't you think she'd have wanted you to go on?"

No. She hadn't really cared if he'd lived or died. All she'd cared about was where she was going to get her next hit of heroin. "It doesn't matter. I know what's best for me."

"I guess we'd all like to think we do," she said.

"If we don't, who does?"

"Sometimes it's difficult for us to see ourselves as clearly as others can see us."

She was probably right. But he didn't want her looking too closely at him. Otherwise, she'd see that he had a hole, a big, dark hole, all the way down to his soul. "Is that Liz or Liz the psychologist talking?"

She looked a little offended. His goading tone had done what he'd intended. "I'm not sure I can separate Liz from Liz the psychologist. It's who I am."

For the hundredth time, he was glad he'd managed to put on the brakes at the cabin. She deserved better. Better than some guy who was so afraid of losing what he loved that he wouldn't love at all. He didn't need a damn psychologist to explain it to him. "Well, I'm hot and hungry. Let's keep going."

## Chapter Eleven

The next morning, Liz woke up with the birds. They were singing outside her window, welcoming the new day with their high-pitched tune of joy. She turned over, reached out her hand and with one finger separated the blinds. The bright sun made her squint her eyes.

Darn it. She'd overslept. They should have been on the road two hours ago. Why hadn't Sawyer woken her up? Was it possible that he'd overslept, too? Swinging her legs over the edge of the bed, she grabbed a pair of shorts from her suitcase and slipped into them, stuck her feet into her sandals and left the room.

Sawyer's bed was empty. The bathroom door stood half-open, telling her that he'd left the cabin. She made a quick trip to the small room and felt immeasurably better after having brushed her teeth and washed her face. She walked out of the cabin, saw her car and wondered where Sawyer might be.

Maybe he'd gone to the office for coffee today. Oh, she wished she had a gun. She'd love to just shock the heck out of him. He'd open the door, and maybe she'd shoot at his feet just to give him a taste of his own medicine. And then she'd kiss the heck out of him again.

As delightful as that sounded, with nothing more threatening than a nail file, Liz tossed that option. Still, the coffee sounded good. She walked across the parking lot to the office and helped herself to a large black coffee. She passed on the sweets. A few more days of pecan rolls and she'd be one big roll.

On her way back, she discovered Sawyer almost hidden behind the cabin. He was doing push-ups. She didn't know how many he'd done before she started watching, but she saw him do thirty. Then he flipped over onto his back and started in on the sit-ups.

Her throat went dry. The man had on a pair of loose cotton shorts but no shirt. Sweat clung to his skin, and the sun glinted off his broad chest. With each sit-up, the muscles in his stomach rippled. A hundred sit-ups later, he collapsed on his back, his legs spread.

She felt a bit like a voyeur.

When Sawyer sprang up from the ground in one fluid motion, she realized she must have sighed.

"Liz?"

"Good morning," she said. "I'm sorry. I didn't mean to disturb you." *Or stop you.*

"No problem. I needed to stretch out a bit."

"We have spent a lot of time in a car lately."

"Yeah."

Okay. If he could pretend that she hadn't been staring at him, she could, too. "I'm sorry I slept so late."

"You must have needed it."

"Right. Do you want to shower first or should I?"

"You go ahead. I'm going to run for a little while. Just around the parking lot. The cabin won't be out of my sight."

She wondered if she stood on her tiptoes if she could catch a glimpse out the bathroom window. Sawyer was being vigilant in protecting her. She was just being greedy. "Well, I'll see you in a few minutes, then."

He nodded.

By the time she'd showered and dressed and Sawyer had done the same, she felt almost calm. Not at all like a woman who had almost thrown herself on a sweaty, half-naked man in a hotel parking lot.

They drove into town and grabbed a quick breakfast at one of the local eateries. Back in the car, Liz spread the map across her lap. She looked at it then folded it.

"What's wrong?"

"Nothing. I figure you know where you're going."

"I do. South. Then we'll work our way back up on the other side."

It sounded an awful lot like yesterday and the day before. A day of stops and starts and disappointments. Liz resisted the urge to pound her head against the window.

As if Sawyer had read her mind, he asked, "You up for this? We can always go back to the city."

Giving up wasn't an option. Being late had grave consequences. These were the lessons she'd learned. "No, let's go. The sooner we get started, the sooner we find them."

To his credit, Sawyer didn't even respond. He just started driving.

By the middle of the afternoon, Liz felt horrible. She'd worn her most lightweight shirt and shorts, but still the material clung to her skin. It had to be ninety-five degrees in the shade. They'd already stopped at seven campgrounds, two parks and four small motels that crowded the river.

"Next stop is Twin Oaks Lodge," Liz said, holding the map a couple inches off her legs. If she let it rest, it would probably stick to her.

"Yeah, that sounds right. I actually tried to get a cabin there, but they were full. Said they book up by the beginning of April for the whole summer."

"Not a bad position to be in," Liz said.

"It's not all gravy. They have long, cold winters up here," Sawyer reminded her.

"So? We have long, cold winters in Chicago."

With that, he turned the wheel, pulling the car into the large parking lot of Twin Oaks Lodge.

As usual, he pulled off to the side, out of view of the office windows. His cell phone buzzed just as Liz opened her door. He scanned the text message.

"Is it work? Is it Mary?" Liz asked.

"It's work, and I don't know if it's Mary."

"If it's Mary…"

"Then I'll tell you what I can. I just have to respect the privacy and the security of the person who's calling me. Even having you listen in on one side of the conversation could jeopardize that. I won't do that to this person."

"This person? I can't even know if it's a man or a woman?"

"No. Better for you and better for the person."

She nodded, apparently realizing he wasn't going to budge. There was a lot he probably should apologize for, but this wasn't one of the things.

"Fine. I'm going to go into this office, ask my questions and pretend to look at the brochures. If I—" she paused for effect "—would happen to get us both a cold drink, will you promise not to shoot me when I come back?"

It took him a minute to realize that she was kidding, that she was in some way trying to smooth things out between the two of them. He shrugged. "It depends. Make sure it's a diet."

"It's always the details that get a person into trouble, isn't it?" Liz opened the car door and walked across the parking lot. He watched her until she got inside.

He dialed Rafael Fluentes. The man had infiltrated the organization deeper than any other undercover cop had been able to. His calls rarely meant good news.

"It's me," Sawyer said when Fluentes answered.

"I hear you're working the river. How's the fishing?"

"Nobody is biting."

"Sucks everywhere. There's talk of a rumble," Fluentes said.

Damn. It was an unusual night when there wasn't an intergang slaying. Turf battles waged fierce and frequent. Fluentes wouldn't have called about that. This must be a big-time, bring-out-your-big-guns war call. "When?" Sawyer asked.

"Soon."

Sawyer regretted being two hundred miles away. Robert would keep him informed, but it wasn't the same as being there. "Hope the fish bite better there."

"Yeah, me, too. I don't care if the small ones slip through our nets, but I'd like to hook a few of the big ones. By the way, I've got a little info on the sister fish. Mirandez is the only child of Maria and Ramon Mirandez. However, Maria had a child ten years before she married Ramon. We're not even sure Ramon knew about the kid. In any event, Mirandez has a much older half sister out there somewhere."

Maybe that made some sense. She'd come to Mirandez's father's funeral. If Ramon Mirandez hadn't known about the child, Maria Mirandez would have finally been free to have both her children with her to comfort her in her time of need.

"What's her name?"

"Angel."

"Angel what?"

"I don't have a last name. Maria's maiden name was Jones."

"Jones?" Sawyer frowned at the phone.

"Yeah. Mirandez's grandfather was as white as you and me."

"Bet that's not well-known in the hood."

"Remind him of it when you arrest him."

"Angel Jones," Sawyer repeated. "Or Angel whatever. She's probably married by now. Where's she live?"

"Not sure. Maria Mirandez moved to one of those independent living centers a couple years ago. A real nice expensive one."

Sawyer couldn't help but interrupt. "Guess what's paying for that?"

"I know. If we didn't have the drug money, the economy would be in real danger. Anyway, we got one of her old neighbors to talk. She remembers Maria visiting a daughter who lived up north."

"Up north?" Sawyer repeated, even more discouraged than before. "That's it? That's all you got?"

"Maria evidently never drove at night. She could get from her daughter's place to home all in daylight. So, I'm guessing it's not Alaska."

"You're funny."

"Hey, I said it wasn't much. But at least we know there's a sister."

"Yeah, I know. I'm sorry. I'm just getting discouraged."

"Patience is the fisherman's friend. Try to remember that," Fluentes said before he hung up.

Sawyer wouldn't brag about catching Mirandez. But he would get some real pleasure out of seeing him stuffed and mounted on a plaque and hung on somebody's wall. Not his. He didn't want to look at the son of a bitch every day.

He'd been off the phone for three minutes before Liz came out of the office. She was carrying two big cups. She got in and handed him one. He opened the straw, poked it into the hole and took a big drink. "I like a woman who can follow directions."

"Just tell me what to do and I can do it."

She hadn't meant it to be provocative. He could tell that by the sudden blush on her face. But the double meaning hadn't been lost on either one of them. He rubbed his jaw, and his whole damn face felt hot. What a bunch of idiots they were.

"News about Mary?" she asked.

He shook his head. "Mirandez has a sister. A half sister on his mom's side."

"Where?"

"Nobody knows. They'll keep digging. I've got a name. Angel. Might be Angel Jones. Every place we go from now on, we ask for her, too. Maybe we'll get real lucky."

Two STOPS LATER, luck struck. Liz flashed the picture, told her story and waited for the standard answer. When the young man behind the desk gave her a crooked smile and said that she'd be able to find Mr. and Mrs. Giovanni at cabin number seven, she almost wept.

"My sister's pregnant," Liz reminded the clerk, wanting so desperately to believe but knowing she couldn't be too optimistic.

"I know. I was surprised when her husband told me that the baby wasn't due for another couple of months. They wanted to rent a boat yesterday, and I was nervous as heck. Thought she'd probably pop that kid out when she hit the first wave. But they docked it back in last night, safe and sound. Although I don't think your brother-in-law knows much about fishing. Your sister had to show him how to bait a hook."

"Yes, she's a talent. Well, I can't wait to see them. My car is in the parking lot. If I just keep driving on this road, will it take me past cabin seven?"

"Sure thing. And if they aren't there, look for them out at the dock. That's where they seem to spend most of their day. She reads books, and he throws his line in the water and spends most of the day on his cell phone. That's not how I'd spend my vacation. But since your brother-in-law tips twice as good as anybody else, I ain't gonna judge."

Easy to tip when it was with dirty money.

"Well, I'm going to try to surprise them. You won't call them or anything, will you?"

"Couldn't if I wanted to. Cabins don't have phones."

"Well, okay, then. I guess I'll see you later."

"Sure. Just make sure your brother-in-law knows how helpful I was."

Liz managed a smile. She walked quickly back to the car, opened the door and slammed it shut before she turned to Sawyer. "They're here. Cabin seven. Mr. and Mrs. Giovanni."

Sawyer's eyes lit up, and his hands clenched the steering wheel. "Giovanni," he repeated.

"Dark hair. Dark eyes. Guess he figured people in Wisconsin wouldn't know the difference between Hispanic and Italian."

"Suppose. It's not like he could have picked Anderson or MacDougal."

"Now what?" They hadn't really ever talked about what would happen if they actually found them.

"We call for backup. Damn, I wish Robert were here."

"What do I do?"

"Stay here. Once I make the call, I'm going in for a closer look. I want to get the layout of the cabin."

"The clerk said they might be down at the lake. There's a path that runs behind all the cabins."

"Okay. Thanks."

"I don't want Mary getting hurt. You need to let me get her out of there."

"You're not going anywhere near Mirandez. He'll kill you. Without hesitation, without second thoughts."

"But—"

"But nothing," he said. "Don't fight me on this, Liz. I've

been straight with you all along. This is a police operation. You have to stay here. You have to stay safe."

She didn't intend to give up that easily. "You'd have never found her if it wasn't for me. Why can't I just go look around with you?"

"No. Mirandez is a crazy man. Look, Liz, I'll do my best to make sure Mary doesn't get hurt. You've got to trust me."

She would trust him with her life. If Capable Sawyer couldn't handle the trouble, the trouble had a destiny. But she couldn't walk away from Mary now. Not when she was this close.

"It's not a matter of my trusting you. Mary doesn't trust you. She doesn't like you. She's not going to listen to you. She'll do something stupid."

He seemed to consider that. "You'll do exactly what I tell you to do?"

"Yes."

"You won't call out to her or say anything until I give you the sign?"

"No."

Sawyer shook his head as if he couldn't believe what he was about to do. "All right. But don't make me regret this." He picked up his cell phone and dialed the number he'd evidently memorized. He gave the party on the other end a terse description of their location and the suspected location of Mirandez and Mary. He listened for a minute, responded with a terse yes and hung up.

"Who was that?"

"Miles Foltran. He's the sheriff of Juneau County. I made contact with him before we left Chicago so that he knew we were in the area. He'll have backup here in ten minutes."

"Now what?" Liz asked.

"I never should have listened to Fischer," Sawyer muttered.

"What?"

"Never mind. Just be quiet. I need to think."

Liz wasn't even offended. The man had more on his mind than being polite to her.

"Now we go take a look," he said, starting the car. He threw it into Drive and slowly eased out of his parking spot.

"Shouldn't we wait for backup?"

"We are. We're going to keep a nice safe distance away."

Sawyer drove down the narrow blacktop road, keeping his speed around twenty. They saw the first cabin and then ten or twelve more look-alikes. Sawyer continued past cabin seven, all the way until a stand of evergreens took over where the road stopped. He turned his car around, angling it so that he could get a view of the shorefront that ran behind the cabins.

"I don't believe this." Sawyer reached between the seats and pulled out his gun.

"What?" Liz craned her neck to see.

"Look between those two cabins, about a hundred yards out. That's Mirandez."

A short, thin man, wearing a baggy white T-shirt and blue jean shorts that fell below his knees, paced up and down the dock. He had a beer in one hand and a phone in the other.

"Keep talking," Sawyer muttered. "Keep talking, you bastard."

But almost as if that had been the kiss of death, Mirandez lowered his arm, snapped the cell phone closed, walked over to the lawn chair at the edge of the water, held out his hand and helped Mary pull herself out of the chair.

"Mary," Liz murmured, more scared now than ever that she'd actually seen Mary. "You've got to make sure she doesn't get hurt," Liz said. "Promise me."

"Damn," Sawyer said, totally focused on Mirandez. "They're leaving."

Liz stared at the young couple. Sure enough, Mary and

Mirandez were walking toward the black SUV that was parked almost on the sand. Mirandez evidently hadn't wanted his vehicle far from him.

Before she could even think about what to do, Sawyer threw the Toyota into Drive and pulled up to the end of the driveway. "Get out now. My side."

He opened the door, stepped out, grabbed her arm and literally pulled her from the car. He gave her a quick, hard kiss. "Run like hell for the trees."

"What are you doing?"

"What I ain't gonna do is let the bastard get away. He can't get around me. He's going to have to go through me. Now get the hell out of here."

LIZ HEARD MIRANDEZ's SUV engine kick to life, and she knew she had mere seconds. "Mary," she managed to choke out.

Sawyer spared her a quick glance. "I'll do the best I can."

She ran for all she was worth, reaching the trees just when she heard the horn. Mirandez leaned on it, obviously irritated that someone had the audacity to block his way. Liz could see him looking around, and she prayed that he wouldn't see either her in the trees or Sawyer, who had somehow managed to get behind a big oak tree about twenty yards to the left of the car.

When she heard the scrunch of car on car, she knew that Mirandez had gotten tired of waiting. With the bumper of his SUV, he pushed the rear of her car aside. In another fifteen seconds, he'd have enough space to squeeze out.

And almost as if in slow motion, Sawyer stepped out from the tree, fired twice, hitting the front wheel of the SUV. Mirandez reached his arm out of the open window, a deadly-looking gun extended from his hand, and fired at Sawyer, who had slipped once again behind the tree.

Liz wanted to scream but knew she couldn't distract Sawyer. The bullets bounced off the tree, the only protection Sawyer had against the horrible gun. Liz, almost without thought or intent, grabbed some rocks from the ground, and with all her strength, she flung them across the road, straight toward the cabin. One hit the door, another the roof and the rest scattered across the ground.

It was enough to momentarily distract Mirandez, and Sawyer didn't miss his opportunity. With Mirandez's attention on the cabin, Sawyer swung his big frame out from behind the tree.

The bullet caught Mirandez's forearm, and his gun fell to the ground.

Sawyer ran to the SUV, kicked the gun a hundred feet, all the while keeping his own gun leveled at Mirandez's head. "Police," Sawyer announced. "Turn off the engine."

Mirandez looked up, maybe to judge his chances, and Liz held her breath. Then, with a slight shake of his head, as if he couldn't believe what was happening, he turned off his vehicle.

"Mary, get out of the car," Sawyer instructed, his voice steady.

For just the briefest of seconds, Mary didn't move. Then she almost tumbled out in her haste.

Liz met her halfway. She reached for her and held her as close as the pregnancy allowed. She thanked God. They'd found her in time. This time she hadn't been too late.

Mirandez screamed and yelled obscenities at Sawyer. But when Sawyer took a step toward Mary, Mirandez changed tunes.

"Get the hell away from my baby," the drug dealer yelled. "You don't have any right. I'll kill you. I swear to the Holy Mother that you're a dead man."

*His baby.* Liz pulled away from Mary, wiping a gentle hand across the girl's teary face. What the heck was going on?

"Oh, Liz," Mary cried, "I was so scared. I didn't think I'd ever see you again. I—"

Just then, four squad cars rounded the corner. Six officers piled out, guns drawn.

"I'm a police officer," Sawyer called out. "The man in the SUV is Dantel Mirandez. He's wanted on suspicion of murder."

The tall one in the front of the pack held his hand up in the air, motioning those behind him to stop. "Detective, your voice sounds about right. But given that I've only talked to you on the phone, put your gun down now and show us some ID."

Sawyer nodded. "That's fine. Come a little bit closer. If he moves, shoot him. He dropped his gun. It's to my right, twenty-five feet out."

Sawyer laid his own gun on the ground and watched while the officers secured Mirandez's gun. He unclipped the badge on his shirt pocket that he'd hastily attached right before he'd pushed Liz from the car and run for cover himself. He tossed it at the man who'd spoken.

The man glanced at it for a moment, and then a big grin spread across his face. "Welcome to Wisconsin, Detective Montgomery. Looks like you've had quite a day."

Sawyer thought he might have the same silly-ass grin on his own face. "Watch him," he warned again before he picked up his gun and put it back in the car. Then he strode over to Liz and Mary.

"You both all right?" he asked.

"We're fine," Liz answered.

Sawyer took a long look at Mary. She looked tired and pale, and she was holding on to Liz so tightly that he was surprised Liz could still breathe. "What's the story here, Mary?"

"He's a monster," Mary answered, her voice brimming with tears.

"Did he hurt you?" Sawyer asked. "The baby?" Suddenly he knew killing Mirandez wouldn't be enough. He'd have to torture him first.

Mary shook her head and took a couple of loud sniffs. "Dantel has a sister who lives around here. She's a nurse. They were going to cut me up. And then take my baby."

"What?" Liz asked.

"But they had to wait. His sister said I had to be at least thirty-six weeks so that the baby would be big enough."

"But aren't you almost thirty-eight weeks, honey?" Liz brushed her hand gently over Mary's hair.

"Yeah. But he didn't know that. He was gonna keep me up here until his sister thought I was ready."

"It's not his baby, is it?" Sawyer asked. Liz had been right. Suddenly it was all starting to make some sense. "But he thought it was."

"Dantel treated me like a queen, bought me anything I wanted, took me anywhere I wanted to go. I couldn't tell him I was already six weeks pregnant before we ever slept together."

More lies. When would the damn lies stop? Sawyer pushed the disgust back. "He wants the baby?"

"His mother is dying. She wants a grandchild before she dies. His sister can't have any kids."

Sawyer wanted to make some sick joke about Mirandez being a mama's boy. But he couldn't. Dying mothers weren't funny. "How'd you find out what he had planned?"

"I didn't know at first. When we left Chicago, he said that he just wanted to get away and relax for a few days. I didn't want to go but you...you can't turn Dantel down. He doesn't like it."

Sawyer bet not. "Then what?"

"I thought we were going fishing. But he didn't have a

clue what he was doing. I started getting scared. There isn't even a phone in the room."

"What happened?"

"We went to his sister's house. At first she was really nice, talking to me about the baby and everything. But then I had to pee so I went upstairs to the bathroom. When I came down, I heard her telling Dantel that it would be a couple weeks before she could take the baby. That she didn't want to take a chance on the lungs."

The devil seed had taken root and sprouted in the Mirandez family. "Then what?" Sawyer asked.

"I pretended that I didn't hear them. I ate dinner with that horrible woman and pretended that nothing was wrong. I thought I might have a chance to get away. Dantel had been on the phone all the time. Another gang issued a challenge. There's going to be a big fight soon."

"Where?" Sawyer asked. "Did you hear him say where and when?"

"Yes. Maplewood Park. On Sunday night."

"Good girl," Sawyer said. "That information is going to be very helpful."

"Dantel hated that he wasn't in Chicago to control things. He went crazy on the phone one night, talking to somebody. I thought it might be my chance. But he saw me. I told him I stepped outside for some air, but I knew he didn't believe me. Since then, he's been watching me like a hawk." Her lower lip trembled, and a fresh set of tears slid down her face.

The girl had a lot of guts. "You did good," Sawyer told her. "You saved yourself and your baby. You should be proud."

When Liz threw him a grateful glance, Sawyer felt his heart, his stone-cold heart, heat up just a bit.

He was about to do something stupid like thank her when Sheriff Foltran interrupted him. "We've read him his rights, Detective. He needs medical attention. We'll see that he gets that at the local emergency room, and then we'll get him booked. My friend Bob owns this place, and I don't think he'll appreciate us hanging around until all his other guests show up."

Sawyer nodded at the man. "Right. Put him in one of your cars. I'll ride with you." He turned back to Liz and Mary. "I'm going to have to deal with this. He crossed state lines, so it's a bit more complicated to get him back into our jurisdiction. And then I need to arrange secure transport back to Chicago."

"How long will that take?" Liz asked.

"Probably a day or so. You two can go back now. Take the car. I think it will still run."

"It's over?" Mary asked.

"This part is over. I still need your testimony."

Mary nodded. "I want the bastard to pay. He was going to let that woman cut my baby out."

"You'll testify about the murder you saw?"

Mary didn't say anything for a full minute. She just stared at the ground. Then she looked at Liz. "Dantel said he'd kill me," she said, her voice very soft. "He said he'd kill you, too. He sent you that letter just to scare you. And he shot up your office just so we'd both know he was serious and that he could get to us anytime he wanted. He had the bomb put there, too. I don't know how but he did it. I'm so sorry."

"It's okay," Liz assured her. "He'll be in jail."

God willing, Sawyer thought. God and a smart jury. His gang would still be on the prowl. Sawyer wondered if Liz had any idea the risk Mary was taking. He should tell her.

"He beat that man and killed him," Mary said. "He was laughing while he did it. The guy was screaming and crying, and there was blood everywhere."

Hell, maybe he ought to do everybody a favor and manage to drop Mirandez in the Wisconsin River. With a fifty-pound sack of cement around his neck.

But he wouldn't. Even given the number of times he'd seen the system fail the community it served, Sawyer still believed in it. Believed that if he did his job right, the next guy would do the same, and so on. It was what separated them from the animals, both the four-legged and the two-legged like Mirandez.

Right now what he wanted most in the world was to take Liz into his arms. But he knew that couldn't happen. Even with Mirandez in custody, it wouldn't be fair to Liz to pursue a relationship. He didn't intend to offer marriage. He couldn't offer children. He needed to make a clean break of it now.

"I'm going to be pretty busy for a few days. He'll need to be processed."

Liz nodded.

"I need your written statement," Sawyer said to Mary.

"Now?"

"That would be best." He pulled the ever-present notebook out of his shirt pocket.

"Don't I have to sign a form or something?"

"You write it, date it and sign it. I've accepted statements written on crumpled-up paper towels. It doesn't matter what it looks like. What matters is what it says."

Mary assessed him for a long moment. "You know, you're not so bad for a cop."

Didn't rank up there with Liz looking at him as if he walked on water but it still made him feel real fine. "You're not so bad yourself. What are you two going to do when you get back to town?"

Mary was back to her shrugging.

Liz saw it, too. "Mary, I want you to stay with me. For at least a couple of days."

He didn't miss the pure relief that crossed Mary's face.

It reminded him of how much of a kid she really was. That didn't stop him from wishing that Liz hadn't made the offer. Mary attracted trouble. He didn't want Liz getting caught in the cross fire. He wouldn't be there to protect her.

"Your car should drive fine even though Mirandez did dent it up a little. I'm going to call Robert and ask him to meet you at your apartment. Just to make sure it's still secure."

"What?" Liz looked at him as if he'd lost his mind.

"I think we have a good chance that the judge will deny Mirandez bail. He's clearly a flight risk. We'll keep the lid on the fact that Mary's going to put him in the hot seat. Given that he still thinks Mary's pregnant with his baby, she's probably safe for now. You, too. But I don't want to take any chances. I'd feel better if Robert meets you there."

"Oh."

He knew immediately that if it were just her, she'd argue until she turned blue. But she wouldn't take a risk with Mary.

"You remember him, right?"

She nodded. "It's just a bit embarrassing."

"What?"

"The last time I saw Robert, I wasn't exactly dressed for success."

Sawyer remembered exactly how she'd been dressed. Or mostly undressed. He'd bet his last dime Robert did, too. "He won't even mention it." Sawyer would make damn sure of that.

## Chapter Twelve

Liz was an hour from home when her cell phone rang. She answered it, keeping one hand on the wheel. "Hello."

"Everything okay?"

She'd left Sawyer more than two hours ago. Capable Sawyer clearly didn't like having things out of his immediate control and he probably figured he was due an update. "We're fine. No trouble."

"Good," he said.

The relief in his voice made her insides do funny little jumps. *Slow down, girl. He's a cop. With a misguided sense of responsibility.*

"I called Jamison and told him everything," Liz said. "Now that Dantel Mirandez is in police custody, he wants to reopen OCM, especially since we know Mirandez sent that letter to me. Do you have any concerns about that?"

Sawyer didn't answer right away. When he did, he didn't sound too happy. "I guess not," he said. "There's always some risk. But I don't think we can expect the man to keep his business closed forever."

"He'll be glad to hear that."

"I suppose you're planning on going back right away?"

"Of course. Why wouldn't I?"

He sighed. "By the way, I talked to Robert. Pull into the alley behind your building. He'll meet you there."

"Okay."

"If you don't see him right away, don't get out of the car. Just keep driving until you get to the closest police station. And call me."

"I'm sure everything will be fine."

"I know. It just doesn't hurt to have a plan B."

She imagined Capable Sawyer always had a plan B. "Mary has slept most of the way."

"That's good. By the way, I read her statement again. She did a good job. Lots of detail that will be helpful. Just remember, when she wakes up, remind her not to tell anyone that Mirandez isn't the father. That's the best protection she has right now."

"What happens when she delivers within a couple weeks and it's obvious the baby is full-term? What happens if Dantel tries to claim that he's the father?"

He didn't answer right away. When he did, he surprised her. "If Mary's telling the truth, a simple blood test will rule out Mirandez's claim. Of course, then her life won't be worth the paper that the test is printed on. When Mirandez finds out that she's going to testify against him, she's going to be in real trouble."

"What is she going to do?"

"She's going to have to get out of town, Liz."

"Are you crazy?"

"No. Don't say anything to her yet. I don't want her freaking out."

Liz gave Mary a quick glance. The girl snored, her head at a strange angle against the headrest.

"Well, I'm freaking out. She hasn't signed adoption paperwork yet. What if she decides to keep her baby? She can't just go off on her own with a newborn. She's going to need help."

"That can be arranged."

Liz realized with a sinking heart that he'd had time to

think it through. He'd known from the moment Mary confessed that this was how it had to end. Liz stepped on the gas a bit harder, wishing it was his head. "You should have told her. Before she confessed that she'd been there. You should have told her that her life would never be the same again."

"We need her. She's the one who can put Mirandez away. I never pretended anything—"

"But leaving town?" Liz interrupted. "That's huge. It means…it means I'll never see her again."

There, she'd said it. She didn't want to lose Mary.

For a minute, she thought he'd hung up. There was absolutely no noise on the other end of the phone. When he did speak, he sounded a bit strange. "Liz, I'm sorry. I probably should have said something. I couldn't. I just couldn't give Mary a reason to not do the right thing. A man died that night. Mirandez killed him, and he needs to pay for that. I know this is tough. But Mary would have drifted out of your life sooner or later. This way you'll know she's safe."

She absolutely hated that he made sense.

She wanted to hang on to her anger, to somehow let it soothe the pain of loss. But really the person to be angry at was Dantel Mirandez. It wasn't Sawyer's fault. "So, this is real-life witness-protection stuff?"

"Yeah. It doesn't just happen on the television shows."

"She's not going to take this well."

"Don't tell her yet. I just wanted you to have a chance to hear it first. When I get back to town, we'll tell her together."

She let up on the gas, and her stomach started doing those funny little jumps again. "Thank you, Sawyer." It sounded awfully inadequate, but she couldn't yet verbalize her feelings. They were too fresh, too unexpected, too much.

"It'll be okay, Liz. I promise. Just trust me on this one."

"I've always trusted you, Sawyer." *Even before I loved you.*

She jerked the wheel when the right-side tires swerved off the highway.

She felt hot and cold and sort of dizzy. "Traffic's picking up," she said. "I've got to go."

"Okay. Be careful. Please."

*Careful?* It was a little late for that. She'd fallen in love with Sawyer Montgomery.

Forty-five minutes later, she pulled into the alley and found her regular parking space. She'd barely turned the car off when someone tapped on her window. Even though she'd been expecting Detective Hanson, she still jumped several feet.

He smiled at her, but when a blue car pulled into the alley and headed toward them, his smile and easy demeanor vanished. "Get as close to the other door as you can. Lie down on the seat," he ordered.

Liz did as she was told, grateful that Mary still slept, slumped down in the seat. She saw that Detective Hanson had left the car door open and moved behind it. He had his gun out.

Liz held her breath and waited for the shots. All she heard was the engine of a car badly in need of a tune-up. It sounded as if it never even slowed down as it went past.

"It's okay." Detective Montgomery stood up. "Two old ladies. Both with blue hair."

Liz laughed. "Not part of Mirandez's gang?"

"I doubt it." He looked at Mary. "She sleep all the way here?"

"Yes. I don't think she's had much sleep the past couple of days."

"Let's get her inside. Street is pretty quiet. I've been here for about fifteen minutes and haven't seen anything unusual. I don't expect any trouble."

"Okay. Mary." Liz leaned over to tap the girl on her shoulder. "Wake up, sweetie. We're home."

Mary's eyes fluttered open. She looked at Liz first, then at Detective Hanson. "Who are you?" she asked.

"Detective Robert Hanson."

"Oh, yeah. I remember you. You were with Detective Montgomery. I guess you're the babysitter?"

Detective Hanson didn't look particularly offended. "I'll bet you can't wait for my microwave popcorn."

Mary snorted.

He ignored it. "Let's go," he said. "Stay close. Do what I tell you to do when I tell you to do it."

Liz knew the past several days had taken their toll on Mary when she didn't argue with Robert.

They got inside without incident. Robert checked each of the rooms. Mary stood in the kitchen, waiting for him to finish. When he did, she gave Liz a hug and went off to sleep in the spare bedroom. Liz gave her an extra blanket and shut the door behind her. Then she sank down onto her couch, loving the feel of the leather fabric. It was good to be home.

"Can I ask you something, Ms. Mayfield?" Detective Hanson asked. He stood near the kitchen counter. "How is Sawyer?"

"Stubborn. Bossy. Opinionated." She held up three fingers and ticked off the list.

Robert rubbed his hands together. "I knew it. I knew it from the first day I saw the two of you together. Like a match and dry kindling."

"Oh, but we're not…" She stopped, unwilling to share the private details of her relationship.

Robert laughed. A quiet chuckle. "Well, I hope you are soon. Otherwise, he's going to be a real pain in the ass to work with."

WHEN THE PHONE RANG late that night, Liz practically vaulted off the couch. The apartment had gotten very quiet after Robert had left and Mary had gone to bed. "Hello?"

"Ms. Mayfield?"

She didn't recognize the voice. "Yes."

"This is Geri Heffers from Melliertz Hospital. Melissa Stroud asked me to call you. She had a baby girl tonight."

Melissa. She wasn't due for another week. "Is everything okay?"

"Everything's fine. I understand you're Melissa's counselor and that you've been helping her arrange for an adoption. She's going to be released the day after tomorrow."

Liz knew what that meant. Melissa needed to sign the paperwork before she left the hospital. According to state law, she'd have seventy-two hours to change her mind. The baby would either stay in the hospital or be released to temporary care in a foster home until that time period elapsed. Only then could she go to the adoptive parents.

"I'll be there tomorrow. I'll come late afternoon." Liz promised the nurse and hung up. She dialed Howard's number from memory.

When he answered, she didn't waste words. "Howard, it's Liz. Melissa Stroud had her baby today at Melliertz. It's a girl. Healthy. She wants to sign papers tomorrow. Can you meet me there around four in the afternoon?"

"Excellent. The Thompsons really wanted a girl."

"The Thompsons? I thought Mike and Mindy Partridge were the adopting parents."

"No, they wanted to wait another couple months. Mike's traveling a lot these days."

"Have I met the Thompsons?"

"No. But they're great. I've done a full background check. You couldn't ask for better. I've talked to Jamison about them."

She didn't like it when she hadn't met the adopting parents. This had happened before. But when she'd mentioned something to Jamison, he'd told her not to worry about it and that he trusted Howard's judgment. "I'd like to see the background report," she said.

"Oh, sure," Howard said. "I'll bring it with me to the hospital."

Liz hung up the phone and went to check on Mary. She'd been right. It looked as though Mary would sleep through the night. The pregnancy, the worry, it had worn out the young girl.

Liz wished for just a bit of Mary's sleepiness. She turned on the television. Ten minutes and bits and pieces of three sitcoms later, she turned it off. She picked up a new magazine that had been waiting for her in the mailbox. Flipping page by page, she got halfway through it before she admitted defeat.

She couldn't stop thinking about Sawyer. What was he doing? Was he still interrogating Mirandez? Had he had dinner? Had he returned to the cabin? Had he gone to bed?

That was where her thoughts got her into trouble. She wondered if he slept in underwear. She didn't have to imagine whether he wore basic white. That little puzzle had been solved when he'd greeted her at the door with a gun and a pair of unsnapped jeans.

She'd been so darn busy looking at his zipper and the equipment underneath that she'd barely given the gun more than a passing thought. She hadn't worried that Sawyer would shoot her. Capable Sawyer didn't make mistakes like that.

Robert thought they were like a match and dry kindling. What he didn't know was that with a few choice words about responsibility and professionalism, Sawyer had effectively doused the flames, looking every bit like a man afraid of fire.

It made her wonder exactly what or who had burned Sawyer in the past. She'd wanted to ask Robert but knew it would be useless. Sawyer was his friend. He would guard his secrets.

Why hadn't Sawyer called? He'd said he *might* call, not that he *would* call. Why would he call? When she picked up a paper and pen, no longer content to silently argue with herself, and actually started to make a list of whys and why nots, she knew she'd gone around the bend.

Nothing would ever be the way it was before she'd met Sawyer. Heck, she'd never even be able to enjoy a big bowl of gumbo again. If she saw flowering vines climbing up a wrought-iron railing, she'd probably burst into tears. She'd never be able to go south of the Mason–Dixon line again.

Liz got up and walked over to the shelf where she kept her favorite CDs she'd purchased years ago. She pulled out two, walked into her kitchen, opened the cabinet door under her sink and dumped them into the trash.

She was done with New Orleans jazz.

She returned to the couch and reached an arm toward the light switch. She might not sleep, but at least she could brood in the dark.

Liz almost slept through her appointment with Howard. She had gotten up once, around nine, and fixed breakfast for Mary. She steered Mary toward the television and then went back to bed. When she woke up the second time, she had a headache, a stuffy nose and a sore throat. As irrational as it was, she blamed Sawyer.

She showered and got dressed as fast as her ailing body allowed. She walked out to the kitchen and poured half a glass of orange juice. Her throat was so sore she knew she'd be lucky to get it down. "You doing okay, Mary?"

"I didn't know you had cable," Mary said, holding the remote control.

"Enjoy. I've got to go meet OCM's attorney. I'll be back by dinner. There are snacks in the cupboard. Help yourself."

Mary waved and flipped channels. Liz left the apartment. Halfway to the hospital, her stomach rumbled with hunger, but unless she could find somewhere that pureed eggs and bacon, she was out of luck.

Howard waited for her outside the front doors of the hospital. When he bent to kiss her cheek, she pulled back. "Don't get too close. I have a sore throat. I'm probably contagious."

When he jumped back a full foot, she couldn't help but compare him to Sawyer. Somehow she just knew that little short of the plague would keep Sawyer Montgomery from kissing his girl.

Oh, God, how she wanted to be that girl.

"You look horrible," Howard said.

"Thank you. I worked all night on this look."

He frowned at her. "If you didn't go gallivanting around the countryside, you'd probably stay a lot healthier."

*Gallivanting?* She'd saved an unborn baby from a crazy woman's knife. She couldn't have a lot of regrets. "Did you bring the background report?" she asked.

Howard put a hand over his mouth. "Oh, no. I completely forgot. Trust me, it's fine. They're great people."

"I'm not comfortable with this," Liz said.

"Come on. We're both here. You don't feel well. You surely don't want to stick around while I run all the way across town to get them from my office. You won't want to come back later. You'll probably be sleeping. So, let's just get this over with."

Unfortunately, everything he'd said was true. "Okay. But fax them to me tomorrow. Please don't forget. I need the information for my files."

After a quick stop at the hospital gift shop to pick up a box of candy, they checked in at the nurses' desk on the Maternity floor. They got the room number and walked down the long hallway. When they got there, they saw Melissa sitting up in her bed, watching a game show.

"Hi, Melissa," Liz spoke softly from the doorway, not wanting to scare the young woman. "How are you?"

"Hi, Liz. I'm okay, I guess."

Liz smiled at her client. Melissa Stroud had graduated from high school just three months earlier. She'd been the valedictorian of her class. Her gown had been big enough that the visitors, all the parents and aunts and uncles and grandparents proudly coming to see their offspring, probably hadn't realized that she was six months pregnant.

They'd have all been shocked that a smart girl like that could have gotten herself in trouble.

The father of the baby had been the salutatorian. First and second in their class.

Two smart kids having dumb sex.

"I've brought Howard Fraypish with me. You've talked to him on the phone."

"Okay."

Liz wasn't worried that the girl didn't show more emotion. Generally, that was how most of the girls got through the adoption process. They simply shut off their feelings.

"How's the baby?" Liz asked.

"Good. The nurses said she was real pretty."

Liz thought she caught just the hint of pride in the girl's voice. "You haven't seen her?"

"No. They said I could. Even after I told them I was giving her away. But I couldn't. I just couldn't." And suddenly, a tear slipped out of Melissa's eye, running down the smooth surface of her eighteen-year-old face.

She brushed it away with the back of her hand. "It's stupid to cry. I'm giving her away. That's what I want. That's what I planned on."

Liz felt her own tears threaten to fall. She blinked her eyes furiously. No matter how right the decision was, it was always painful. "You're a very brave girl, Melissa."

The girl shook her head. "I'm never going to sleep with another boy again as long as I live."

Liz smiled and patted the young girl's arm. "Someday you will meet a fine man. He'll make your heart race and your palms sweat." Just like Sawyer did to her. "The two of you will get married, and you'll have beautiful, brilliant children. Your heart will heal. Trust me."

Melissa sniffed. "It's hard to think about things like that. I hope she understands why I had to do this. I hope she realizes that it wasn't because I didn't love her."

"She'll understand," Liz assured the young girl, whose circumstances had forced her to become mature fast. "After all, she has a very smart mother. She'll understand all kinds of things."

Melissa smiled. "Well, let's get it over with."

Howard pulled up a chair. He opened his briefcase and pulled out a stack of papers. In a matter of minutes, Melissa had officially given away her child.

"Do you want me to stay?" Liz asked.

"I think I'd rather be alone. But thank you. I don't think I could have gotten through this without you."

Liz knew from previous experience that Melissa wasn't through it yet. She'd spend many hours sorting through the myriad of feelings, traveling down the dozens of paths her mind would wander around and through until she came to terms with her decision.

Liz hugged the girl. "I'll call you tomorrow."

Liz took the time to stop at the grocery store on the way home. She was anxious to get back to Mary, especially after seeing Melissa, and she was still feeling as if she'd gotten run over by a bus, but her cupboards were pretty bare. She needed to stock up if she intended to have a houseguest. She knew that Mary should have milk and fruit and vegetables.

Thinking about that reminded her of Sawyer buying her bananas, and she walked through most of the grocery store with tears in her eyes. Lord, she was an emotional mess.

She drove home and lugged her sacks inside. She set them on the floor next to the fridge.

"Mary," she called out. "I got Double Stuf Oreos."

No answer. The television was off. Liz listened for the shower. But nobody was running water in her apartment. In fact, she couldn't hear anything. Her apartment sounded empty. The truth hit her, almost making her stagger backward.

Mary was gone.

## Chapter Thirteen

She ran from the kitchen to the spare bedroom. The bed was sort of made with the sheets and blankets pulled up, just not tucked in. A white sheet of notebook paper lay on the pillow.

It took every ounce of courage that Liz had to close the ten-foot gap. The message was short and sweet.

Liz, thanks for everything. You and that cop saved my life. By the way, he's not such a bad guy. I've talked to an old friend. She's going to let me share her place. I'll call you soon. Love, Mary.

Liz wanted to rip somebody's head off. Either that or sit down and cry for about a week. Or something in between those two extremes. She felt as if she was on a seesaw. She'd been high in the air, and the other person had just jumped off, causing her to hit the ground with a thud. Every bone in her body ached with the pain of betrayal, of abandonment.

She wanted to damn Mary to hell and back.

Why couldn't the girl have stayed put? What possessed her to leave? Why couldn't she just accept Liz's help?

Liz didn't have any answers. All she knew was that she wouldn't be able to rest until she was sure Mary and the baby were safe. She got herself off the floor, walked over to the phone and dialed Sawyer's cell phone. She'd given the number out so many times in Wisconsin that she knew it by heart.

He answered on the third ring. "Montgomery." His voice sounded so good, so solid.

"Sawyer?" she said. "It's Liz."

"What's wrong?" he asked immediately.

She laughed. She couldn't help it. So much for trying to hide anything from Capable Sawyer. "Mary's gone. She left a note."

There was a long silence on the other end of the phone. She realized that Sawyer wasn't surprised. It made her angry with herself that she hadn't seen it coming, as well.

"You're not surprised, are you?" she asked. "That's why you made her write down her statement. You knew she wouldn't be around to do it later."

Another pause, although this one was shorter than the last. "I didn't know," he said. "Not for sure. I had an idea she might run."

"I didn't see it." It broke her heart to admit it. How could she keep her girls safe if she didn't anticipate, if she didn't plan ahead?

"Liz," Sawyer said, "don't beat yourself up. She's a fickle kid."

A kid living in an adult world with adult dangers. "I've got to find her. I've got to know she's okay."

"No! That's crazy talk. You aren't going after her again. You know what happened the last time."

Sawyer's tone no longer held sympathy, but now a warning. A couple weeks ago she'd have taken offense. Now she could hear the caring behind his harsh tone.

"I'll be careful," she said. "I won't do anything foolish."

"You're not listening. You won't do anything. It's over. She's gone. Let her go."

"I can't do that." She knew he didn't understand. Knew that he couldn't. She needed to help him. "Sawyer, I told you that my sister, Jenny, died. What I didn't tell you was that I had the chance to save her."

"What?"

"Two days before she killed herself, Jenny left a message on my machine. 'Call me,' it said. I tried. No one answered. I wasn't worried. She'd left messages like that before. I got home from work the next night, and there was another message. 'Please call me,' it said." Her voice cracked, and she swallowed hard, knowing she needed to get through this.

"Liz, sweetheart, it's okay. You can tell me later."

"No. I need to tell you now. I didn't call. My friend and I had tickets to the opera. I'd left work late. She was already waiting outside my apartment when I got home."

She heard him sigh. It made her want to reach through the phone and hug him.

"I tried first thing the next morning. Couldn't get an answer. I remembered that my parents were out of town for the weekend. So, I drove to the house. You know the rest."

"I'm sorry," he said. "It's not your fault. There's no way you could have known."

"Perhaps not. But what I learned is that people reach out for help in different ways. I don't know if Mary's reaching out. Maybe she's not. Maybe she's pulling away and I'm just scared to let go. But I can't take the chance."

There was a long silence from his end. "Promise me," he said finally. "Promise me that you won't do anything until I get there. I'll leave in fifteen minutes. I won't stop for gas, for dinner, for anything. I'll be at your apartment in three hours."

No doubt about it—Sawyer Montgomery defined good. "I'll wait," she promised.

"Thank you," he said, and then he hung up.

THREE HOURS and twenty-seven minutes later, Sawyer pulled his borrowed car up in front of Liz's apartment building. He owed Sheriff Foltran a case of cold beer. That was the price the older man had quoted.

After Sawyer had hung up with Liz, he'd called him, given him a brief update and asked where he might rent a car. The sheriff had quickly set him straight, telling him that wasn't how it was done in the country. Within fifteen minutes, Sawyer had been on the road in a 2004 Buick, courtesy of the sheriff's wife.

He knocked on Liz's door. "Liz, it's Sawyer."

And when she opened it and walked into his arms, it felt right. He held her close, his chin resting on her head, content to let the heat of her body warm his soul.

"Thanks for coming," she said.

Three simple words. But the way she said it, it didn't seem simple at all. It seemed huge, bigger than life itself. It filled his heart, his whole being.

He bent his head to kiss her.

She jerked back. "I had a really sore throat this morning. It's better, but you still might catch it."

He shook his head. "I don't care." He reached for her again.

She slipped into his arms. "I knew you wouldn't care," she said. "I just knew it." She lifted her lips and kissed him.

He felt as if he'd come home. He wanted to consume her, to take sustenance from her strength, her goodness, her essence.

When he slipped his tongue inside and swallowed her answering groan, he knew, beyond the shadow of a doubt, that life would never be the same.

He kissed her for a very long time then wrapped his arms around her slim body and held her close.

"I missed you," he said.

"I know," she said, her words muffled, her lips pressed against his chest.

"Are you okay?" he asked. He put his fingers under her chin and lifted her face up for inspection. She had her long hair pulled back in a rubber band, and she didn't have a speck of makeup on. She looked pure and sweet and so beautiful.

"I'm fine," she said. "Now that you're here, I'm fine."

His chest filled with something that threatened to overtake him, to humble him, to bring him to his knees. "What happened, sweetheart?"

She grabbed a sheet of notebook paper off the lamp table and handed it to him. He turned it over and read it. "Damn kid," he said.

He noticed Liz didn't bother to defend her. But he doubted that her resolve to find Mary had lessened.

"Any thoughts on where she might be?" he asked.

"I want to go back to the bookstore. On the way here, before she went to sleep, Mary talked about getting more books for the baby. I don't know if that woman will tell me anything, but I have to try."

"Okay. I'll take a ride down there. I'll let you know what I find."

"I'm going with you."

"That's not necessary. You stay here. You don't feel well."

She shook her head. "I need to do something. I can't stay here."

He knew better than to try to argue. She had such strength, such sense of purpose, such commitment to a goal. He respected that. It was one of the things he loved about her.

Loved her. It hit him like a bullet against a Kevlar-lined vest. Bruising him, shaking him, shocking him. No longer sure his legs would continue to hold him, he sat down on the couch, hard.

"Sawyer, are you okay? What's wrong?"

Everything. Nothing. He shook his head, trying to make sense of it. He didn't want to love her. He didn't want to love anybody. If you didn't love, then it didn't hurt when you lost.

He needed air. "Let's get out of here," he said, standing up in one jerky movement.

She cocked her head, clearly not understanding his quick turnaround. Hell, he didn't understand it, either. He didn't understand much anymore.

"Sawyer, you're scaring me," she said.

He scared himself. "Liz, let's go. We're wasting time here."

"Are you sure?" she asked.

Oh, yeah, he was sure. Sure he loved her. Just not sure what to do about it.

He nodded. "Let's go. I'd like to get out of that neighborhood before it gets too late."

Sawyer called Robert from the car. "Hey, partner, where are you?" he asked.

"I'm working," Robert said. "Where the hell are you?"

"I'm working, too. Look, I need you to help me with a little surveillance at the corner of Shefton and Terrance."

"Are you in town? I didn't think you were coming back until tomorrow."

Sawyer looked at Liz. He'd used the hands-free speakerphone because of heavy rush-hour traffic. "My plans changed."

"What's at Shefton and Terrance?" Robert asked.

"There's a porn store on the corner of Terrance."

"That desperate, huh?" Robert laughed at his own joke.

"Funny. Mind your manners," Sawyer said. "I've got a lady in the car."

"Hi, Robert," Liz interjected.

"Hi, Liz," Robert said. "Sawyer, you did say *porn store?*"

Sawyer shook his head. "We'll be there in ten minutes.

Meet us at the corner of King and Sparton—that's two blocks
north of the target. I'll fill you in then."

"Can you give me a hint?" Robert asked.

"Sure. We're looking for Mary Thorton," Sawyer said.
"She's AWOL. The porn store is one of her old haunts. I don't
think it's a trap, but I don't want to take a chance."

Ten minutes later, Robert walked into the porn store while
Sawyer and Liz waited in the car, a block away. He returned
ten minutes later carrying a brown paper sack. They watched
him get into the car. Within thirty seconds, Sawyer's phone
rang.

"Store's empty," Robert said, "with the exception of a
greasy-haired old guy in overalls behind the counter."

"No woman, about sixty with gray hair?" Sawyer asked.

"Not that I saw."

Sawyer looked at Liz. "Maybe Grandma Porn only works
the day shift?"

"At night, she bakes cookies for her grandchildren," Liz
replied.

"Anything is possible," Sawyer said. "When it comes to
Mary, I'm beginning to expect the unexpected."

"Let's talk to the guy in the store. Maybe he knows something."

"Okay. Hey, Robert, we're going in."

"Take money. The guy will probably block the door if
you try to leave without buying something."

Liz pulled a twenty out of her purse and stuffed it into
her shirt pocket. "Thanks, Robert," she said. "By the way,
what did you buy?"

Robert laughed. "None of your business. All you need to
know is that I'll be right outside the back door."

Sawyer pulled his car up in front of the store. When he
and Liz entered, the man never even looked up from watch-

ing the small television behind the counter. Liz could just make out the familiar sounds of CNN.

They walked around the store for a few minutes. Finally, the man looked up. "Can I help you find something?" he asked.

"You must be Herbert," Sawyer said.

Liz wanted to smack herself on the head. She'd completely forgotten that the woman had mentioned her man friend Herbert. But Sawyer hadn't. Once again, he amazed her.

"That's me," the man replied.

"We're friends of Mary Thorton's. She talks about how nice you and Marvis have been to her."

"She's a great girl."

"The best," Sawyer agreed. "In fact, she called this afternoon and left a message on our machine. She said she was back in town after being gone a couple of days."

Liz wondered how he did it. The lies just rolled off his tongue.

"She was in Wisconsin," said Herbert.

"That's what she said. Nice time of year to go north," Sawyer added. "Anyway, she must have been having a blonde moment because she told us to call her later, but she didn't leave a number."

"Let me think." The man rubbed his whiskered chin. "I don't have her number. But Randy's place is just a few blocks from here."

*Randy?* Liz desperately wanted to ask, but Sawyer was on a roll.

"Good enough," Sawyer said. "We bought a stroller for the baby. We might as well deliver it."

Herbert picked up a notepad and scribbled an address on it. He held it in his hands. "You folks need anything as long as you're here?" he asked.

Liz pulled the twenty from her pocket. She walked over

to the stack of boxed condoms. She picked out the brightest, most garish design. She handed Herbert the twenty. "Thanks for asking. These should last a couple days," she said.

She heard Sawyer make a choking sound behind her.

"Keep the change," she said. "We'll tell Mary hello from you."

"You two come back anytime." Herbert handed her the slip of paper.

The phone rang seconds after they got back to the car. "Montgomery," Sawyer answered, leaving the phone on speaker. Liz noted he still sounded a bit hoarse.

"Everything okay?" Robert asked.

"Yeah. We got an address. Follow us."

"No problem. By the way, what's in *your* bag, Liz?"

"None of your damn business," Sawyer said and hung up.

"That wasn't very nice," Liz scolded him.

"When this is over," Sawyer said, his voice barely audible, "when we don't have the shadow of Mary or Mirandez or anything else standing between us, we're going to have a long talk."

The heat from Sawyer's body filled the small car. He wanted her. He might deny it, fight it and condemn himself for it. But he wanted her. "Take it from one who knows," she said, "talk isn't always the answer."

She heard the sharp intake of his breath and knew that he'd gotten her point.

She picked up the sack, opened it and peered inside. "I'm glad I bought a big box," she said, happy to let him chew on that for a while.

ONCE AGAIN, ROBERT COVERED the rear of the building, in the event Mary tried to make a run for it. Liz and Sawyer waited for him to get into position before knocking on the apartment door that matched the address Herbert had given them. When Sawyer gave her a nod, Liz rapped on the door.

"Just a minute," a female voice called from within.

Not Mary's voice. Liz looked at Sawyer and knew that he'd had the same thought. When the door opened, Liz knew why the voice sounded familiar. She looked different, of course, without a couple pounds of makeup on, but Liz recognized her. It was the girl from the bar. The one who had given her the original lead on Mary.

She didn't say anything, just simply stared first at Liz and then at Sawyer.

Liz looked past her. Mary sat on the couch.

"Liz?" Mary maneuvered her pregnant body off the cushions. "How did you find me?"

Sawyer stepped into the apartment. His eyes swept the room. "Anybody else here?" he asked.

"No," both girls answered at the same time.

"Mind if I look around?" Sawyer asked.

"You are such a cop." Mary shook her head at him in disgust. "Look around, peek in the closets, look under the beds. I really don't know what Liz sees in you."

Liz felt the hot heat of embarrassment flow through her. Had the two of them been that obvious?

Sawyer looked as if he couldn't care less that she'd put two and two together and come up with four. "Where's Randy?"

The girl who had opened the door held up her hand. "That's me. With an *i,* not a *y.*"

"That your real name?" Sawyer asked.

"Yeah. My dad wanted a boy. Hey, if he's lucky, he'll get a grandson." She rubbed her stomach and laughed at her own joke. "Of course, he'll never know. I haven't talked to him in two years."

"Her dad's a bigger jerk than mine," Mary interjected.

Liz dismissed the comment. Now wasn't the time to try to deal with it. "Are you all right, Mary?" Liz asked.

"I'm fine. I left you a note," she said.

"You did," Liz acknowledged. "I appreciate that. I was still worried. You hadn't said anything about leaving."

"I didn't have anywhere to go. Then I called Randi, and she said I could stay here."

Liz looked around the room. Not much furniture but clean. The biggest mess was on the couch, where Mary had been sitting. When she'd gotten up, the big bag of chips on her lap had spilled. An open carton of milk, propped against the cushions, tilted dangerously.

"I know what I'm doing, Liz. Getting mixed up with Dantel was stupid. I'm not going to make a mistake like that again. But I can't live with you. I need to take care of myself. I need to prove that I can do it."

Liz didn't answer; she couldn't. She walked over to the couch and moved the milk carton from its precarious position to the lamp table, all while trying to sort out her chaotic thoughts. Chips and milk. A contradiction. Just like Mary. Sweet, yet bitter. Young, yet mature beyond her years. Considerate, yet selfish. Independent, yet so dependent.

Liz knew she needed to take a step back. Hated it, but knew it all the same. Otherwise, she ran the risk that she'd alienate Mary and cause her to cut off ties completely. She looked across the room. Sawyer stood absolutely still, watching her. She wanted to run to him and beg him to help her, to tell her what to do. But she knew she had to make the decision. She had to live with the consequences, good or bad.

"OCM is reopening next week. Will you come see me?" she asked.

Mary nodded. "Sure."

Liz swallowed hard, pushing the tears back. She pointed to the chips. "Eat some vegetables, okay?"

"No problem. Randi fixes broccoli every day. She said that we're going to have smart babies because they're getting lots of folic acid."

"You're both going to have beautiful and smart babies," Liz said. She gave Mary a hug first, then Randi. "Take care," she said. "Call me if you need anything."

She walked out of the apartment, hoping she'd make it to the car before she made a complete fool out of herself. Sawyer didn't say a word, somehow knowing that she needed a few moments of silence to sort out her thoughts.

He picked up the phone and held it to his ear, choosing not to use the speaker. He dialed. "Mary's fine," Sawyer said. "Thanks for your help, Robert."

Sawyer paused, listening. "Yeah, she is," he said. Another pause. "I'm not sure. I'll see you tomorrow." Then he hung the phone up.

"What did Robert have to say?" Liz asked.

Sawyer looked very serious. "He said you were a hell of a woman, and he wondered what I was going to do about it."

"Oh." She knew what *she* wanted him to do about it.

"I'm proud of you," he said.

She hadn't done it for Sawyer. But it felt darn good to hear him say those words. She leaned over toward him and kissed him on the cheek. "Thank you. That means a lot to me."

Sawyer put the car in Drive and pulled away from the curb. Neither of them said a word until they were just blocks from Liz's apartment. "You're awfully quiet," Sawyer said. "Are you sure you're okay?"

"I'm fine," Liz lied, knowing that she wasn't a bit fine. She was needy and wanting, but it had nothing to do with Mary and everything to do with Sawyer. Did she have the guts to tell him? If not now, when? When it would be too late? She'd just have to take the chance.

"I want you to make love to me. Tonight. Now."

Sawyer gripped the steering wheel so tightly that his fingers were white. He didn't say a word.

"Don't tell me it would be a mistake," she said. "Don't tell me that it would be inappropriate. It's all I've been thinking about for days."

"Stop," he said. "We'll be at your apartment in five minutes. Don't say another word until we get there."

It took them eight minutes. During that time, Liz didn't spend time regretting acting on the impulse to tell him. She contemplated all the ways she might make love to him. By the time the car stopped, she was practically squirming in her seat.

Sawyer put the car into Park and with deliberate movements turned off the engine and pulled the keys from the ignition. When he turned toward her, her heart plummeted. Liz knew what he'd done in the eight minutes. He'd figured out a way to tell her no. She could see the answer on his face.

"A man would be half-crazy not to want to take you to—"

"Don't give me your speech," she interrupted, refusing to let him walk away. There was more than one way to get her point across. She leaned over the seat and kissed him on the lips. She ran her tongue across his bottom lip.

She heard the quick intake of breath, and she felt the absolute stillness of his body.

"You want me," she stated.

He didn't deny it. She felt her confidence soar.

"Liz," he said, looking miserable, "I'm sorry. It would be a mistake. I can't give you what you want."

"I think you can," she said, looking pointedly at his zipper, which did little to hide his state of readiness.

He blushed. In her lifetime, she'd never expected to see Sawyer Montgomery blush.

"I can't pretend not to want you," he said. "I can't pretend that I don't go to bed hard at night for wanting you."

He spoke softly, but his words had an icy edge to them. She felt the answering heat pummel through her body, landing right between her legs. "There's no need to pretend," she said.

"You want commitment. You want marriage. I'm not offering that. I can't."

The words seemed torn from his soul. She didn't want him to suffer. She wanted them to celebrate life.

"You didn't bring a ring?" she asked, her voice full of accusation.

"No. Listen, I'm not…"

"Sawyer, I'm kidding. It was a joke."

He held her at arm's length. "I don't understand," he said.

"That's what I wanted from Ted. That's not what I want from you."

He looked a bit shocked, then fury crossed his strong features. He chuckled a dry, humorless noise. "Now, that's sweet," he said. "I'm good enough to sleep with but—"

"Sawyer," she said, "I'm sorry. I said that poorly."

He didn't respond.

She needed him to understand. "You're only the second person that I've ever told about Jenny. I told Jamison when I applied for the job at OCM. I thought he deserved to know what had driven me to his little counseling center. I told you because I wanted to share with you the joy of Jenny's life and the despair of her death. I wanted you to understand that both of those experiences make me who I am today."

"I'm glad you told me," he said.

"I want you to hear the rest. Jenny was a bright spot. For sixteen sweet years, she lit up my life. Since her death, I've been mourning that the time wasn't longer. I should have been celebrating the light."

She put her head against his chest. "People pass in and out of your life. They leave you changed, forever different.

You helped me understand and accept that Mary, too, will pass in and out of my life. I can't control that."

"Damn kid." He said it without malice.

"She's very brave."

"She is," he admitted. "Damn brave kid."

She lifted her head from his chest and looked him squarely in the eyes. Now wasn't the time to duck her head, to hide her feelings. "You're going to pass in and out of my life. You've been honest about that from the beginning. I'm not asking for forever. I'm asking for now."

He looked very serious. "I don't deserve you," he said.

She saw the hunger, the pure need, and knew it matched her own. It gave her courage.

"Take me inside," she urged. "Make love to me."

"I cannot resist you," he said. And then without another word, he opened the door and the two of them tumbled out of the car. He walked so quickly to the building that she almost had to run to keep up. When they got to her door, he took the key. Once inside, he shut the door, flipped the bolt lock and kissed her. Long and hard until both of them struggled for breath.

He moved her so that her back was against the wall. He pressed up against her, his chest against hers, his hips grinding into hers. So strong, so big, so much. She pushed her hands up inside his shirt, running her fingers across his bare stomach. His skin burned, and she could feel the muscles underneath. She traced his ribs and, with the tips of her thumb and index fingers, gently pinched each flat nipple.

He groaned and arched his back.

It made her feel powerful, as if she could tempt him beyond thought. It made her feel in control. But when he pulled away suddenly and grasped the hem of her shirt, she knew how quickly control shifted. "I want to see you," he said. "All of you." He yanked her white T-shirt over her head and ran his fingers across the edging of her bra, then lower, just lightly grazing her nipples. And when they responded to his touch, he bent his head and sucked her, right through the sheer material.

"I've been dreaming of this," he whispered against her skin. "Of what you'd look like in lace. You're more beautiful than I could have ever imagined."

His words, his barely there voice, floated around her, assuring her. But then his mouth was back, first on one nipple, then the other, and she couldn't think at all. His mouth moved across her body, lavishing wet kisses on her warm skin. He nipped at her collarbone, sharp licks of his tongue against her neck, before returning his lips to her mouth to kiss her thoroughly.

He reached behind her, releasing the clasp on her bra. She shrugged out of it, never taking her mouth off his. And when he slipped his warm hands into her shorts and cupped her bottom, pulling her against him, she ground her hips into his.

He pulled her shorts and panties down in one quick jerk. They pooled around her feet. Only then did he tear his mouth away. He stepped back a foot and looked at her. He didn't say a word for a moment, just looked at her. Then he took his hand and ever so lightly, with just the very tips of his fingers, brushed her cheek, tucking a strand of hair behind her ear. He let his hand drift downward, across her breast, then down, lingering just moments on her stomach, stopping just at the apex of her thighs. "You're perfect," he said, his voice soft.

He made her feel beautiful. She moved her feet apart, spreading her legs, inviting him to touch her. But he lifted his hand, moving it to the back of her head, working his fingers into her hair, and gently pulled her mouth to his. He kissed her gently, barely touching her at first, stroking her

lips with his tongue, nipping at her bottom lip. He angled
his lips, thrust his tongue into her mouth and kissed her.

When her knees started to buckle, he swept her up into
his arms. With sure and confident steps, he carried her to
the bedroom. He lay her down on the bed and gently pulled
both her arms above her head. Moving across her body, he
nudged her thigh aside. She spread her legs and he kneeled
between them.

"Oh, my God," he whispered, running his fingers across
her naked body. She shivered, and he gave her a smug smile.
Then he bent down, kissing first one breast then the other.

"I need you." She arched her back, pressing her nipple
into his mouth. She would beg soon.

He sucked her, sending shivers from her breast all the way
to her very core. When he pulled back, he moved his strong
hands under each thigh, pulling her legs wide. He moved his
mouth down her stomach, coming finally to the place where
she needed him most. She forgot about being embarrassed,
forgot about wanting to please him, forgot about being lady-
like, and she simply enjoyed. She took and took from him,
the pressure building inside of her until it burst out of control, the waves of pleasure slamming through her.

He held her. He stretched out next to her and pulled her
close, his arms wrapped around her. With every ounce of
strength she had left, she threw one bare leg over his.

Oh, my God. She'd come apart, and he still had every
stitch of his clothes on. Sensing her distress, he held her
just a bit tighter. "Relax, sweetheart. It'll be my turn soon."

"But that's not fair," she protested, her voice weak.

"You don't have any idea, do you, what it does to a man
to have a woman do that for him? To know that he's brought
her pleasure?"

She realized he sounded just a bit smug.

She let him enjoy it for just a moment, then she reached

up and slipped a hand underneath his T-shirt. When her fingers crossed his nipples, she rubbed the tiny nubs. Breath hissed out from between his lips. He had his eyes closed. She trailed her finger down his stomach, following the line of hair. She ran her fingers across his jeans, tracing the ridge of his erection. He arched his hips off the bed. "Oh, sweetheart. You make me feel like a sixteen-year-old again."

His confession gave her courage. She moved quickly, straddling his hips with her legs. She rubbed against him, and he reached up, stilling her. But she wouldn't be stopped. She pulled his T-shirt up. Then she moved down so that her knees touched his. She unsnapped his jeans and pulled his zipper down slowly. He literally groaned.

"I'm a dead man," he said. She laughed. Then with a sure hand on each side of his hips, she pulled his jeans and briefs down.

She made love to him. Her fingers, her lips, skimmed his body, teasing, caressing. When she wrapped her hand around him, his whole body jerked, coming inches off the bed.

"I want to be inside of you," he said.

"I want that, too," she answered.

With one swift movement, he gently flipped her onto her back. He positioned himself above her and gently pushed himself into her. He held himself back, allowing her body to stretch, to adjust to him.

"Oh," she said.

He kissed her face, soft, gentle brushes of his lips. "It's okay. Just a little bit more."

She forced herself to relax and to take him.

"Perfect," he said, his voice a mere whisper.

And then he started to move. Within minutes, she shattered once again. Barely before she could catch her breath, he pounded into her, faster and faster, until his whole body tensed, and with one last powerful thrust, he exploded inside her.

For long minutes, there was no sound at all in the room. Then, with a sigh, he lifted his weight off her. He kissed her—a long, gentle kiss. Then he carefully pulled away from her, then fell onto his back in a clumsy movement. He threw one bent arm over his forehead. "That almost killed me," he said.

It was hard to keep the smile off her face. Now who was feeling smug? she thought.

"I liked it," she said. "Can we do it again?"

He opened one eye and stared at her. "You liked it? You *liked* it?" he repeated. "People *like* apple pie and long walks on the beach."

"I like cherry pie and long walks in the woods. A lot. But trust me on this—I don't like either one of those things as much as I liked this."

"*This* almost gave me a heart attack."

"I know CPR," she said. She boldly wrapped her hand around him, winking at him when he immediately responded.

"Oh, baby." He flipped her onto her back and proceeded to make her own heart race not once but several times over.

# Chapter Fourteen

Sawyer woke up happy and warm. Liz slept on her side, her naked body wedged up against him, her bare back against his chest. He had an arm wrapped around her, and her breast filled his hand.

He moved just a bit. She stretched in response. He let go of her breast, pulled his arm back and gathered her long hair in his hand and moved it out of the way. Then he gently kissed the back of her neck. "Good morning," he said.

"I'll give you a dollar if you make coffee," she said.

He laughed. "I'll give you five dollars if you make breakfast."

She rolled over and laid on her other side, facing him. "I'll give you my last twenty if you'll make love to me again." She winked at him.

"Your last twenty? What happens then?"

"I'm hoping you'll take pity on the poor. I could be your own personal charity."

He rolled onto his back and pulled her on top of him. "I've been known to be a very generous man in the past. Giving of my own personal assets."

"Donate away, baby," she said.

And he did.

And later—much later—when they finally stumbled into

the kitchen, it was closer to lunch than breakfast. "Be careful," she said.

He thought the warning probably saved him a broken leg. He'd surely have tripped over the piles of soup cans, cereal boxes, pots and pans, glasses, silverware and cleaning products scattered on the kitchen floor.

"I like to clean when I'm nervous," she said. "I had some time to kill yesterday between when Mary left and you arrived."

"Anything left *in* the cupboards?"

She shook her head. "Nope. I'm nothing if not thorough."

"Next time you get really nervous, come to my house. My cupboards haven't been cleaned since I moved in."

"Yuck. Sounds gross."

She started coffee and he started lunch. For the first time in seventeen years, he started to think about a future.

"I'm going to go take a shower," she said.

"Okay." Good. He needed time alone, time to sort out his thoughts.

He loved her. He loved her playfulness, her sense of humor, her dedication to her clients, her willingness to help others. He loved her body.

She had wanted commitment and marriage from another man. She didn't expect it from him. He was, in her words, just passing through. He flipped the grilled cheese with more force than necessary, sending it flying out of the pan. It landed on the counter. He picked it up, dusted it off and returned it to the skillet.

Just maybe, *he* wanted a little commitment.

He opened a can of tomato soup. By the time it was hot, Liz had not only returned to the kitchen but he also had a plan.

"If you don't have anything else to do today," he said

carefully, "I thought we might go to Navy Pier. You like Ferris wheels?"

"I love Ferris wheels. But I can't. I have to get my office organized at OCM. I'd brought a lot of my files here. I'll need them back at work when we reopen."

Okay. She wasn't saying no just to say no. She had a commitment to work. He knew how important her work was to her. That was one of the things that made this perfect.

"You really like your job, don't you?" he asked.

"I love my job. Just like you love yours."

Yeah, Sawyer thought as he poured himself a second cup of coffee. Liz didn't need all those things that he couldn't give. She didn't seem concerned about her biological clock like most of the women he'd met over the years. She'd mentioned wanting children, but that was before. Now she had her career. A job she loved. One that she was passionate about.

He wouldn't get in the way. He'd make sure she understood that he didn't intend to disrupt her work. That he valued her dedication. He'd also make sure she realized they weren't ships passing in the night. He'd convince her that she could have both a career and a relationship with a man.

She'd wanted marriage at one time. He'd give her time to adjust to the idea again, and then once she saw that it could work between the two of them, he'd pop the question.

But for now, he'd give her space. He got up from the table, intending to put the dishes in the dishwasher.

"We didn't use my condoms," she said.

She spoke so matter-of-factly, as if she might be discussing the weather or what to have for dinner. He felt the world tilt, causing all the good and beautiful things that had happened last night to slide together, combining into a dark and ugly mess. He held on to his dirty plate tightly, afraid that he might drop it.

He should tell her now. He should have told her before. But now, if she had questions or concerns, it was the right thing to do.

No. He hadn't had a chance to win her over, to convince her of his love.

"I just want you to know that I think the chances are pretty good that we're safe. But if I'm wrong and I am pregnant, I won't expect anything from you. I can handle it myself."

*Tell her, you fool. Tell her.* "You'll let me know?" he asked.

"Of course. I'd never hide something like that."

*Coward.* "No problem. I'm sure it will be fine. I'll call you later today."

"He's not going to call," Liz moaned, her head resting in her cupped hand. It was late afternoon, and she'd worked like a dog all day, trying to reestablish connections with all her clients.

"It's been five hours," she said, looking at the clock.

Jamison walked past her office. He poked his head in, looking around. "Who are you talking to?"

"Myself."

"Fascinating. By the way, Sawyer called."

"What?"

"You must have been on your phone. It rolled over to my line. I told him you'd call him back."

"Oh." She'd been waiting all day, and now that he'd finally called, she didn't know what she was going to say to him.

"Snap out of it, girl," Jamison said. "Just remember. Play a little hard to get. It'll make you more interesting."

"Really?"

"I read it in one of Renée's magazines."

She was about ready to try anything. She picked up the phone and dialed.

"Montgomery."

"Hi, Sawyer. It's Liz."

"Hi. Thanks for calling. Is this a bad time?"

"No, it's fine. Jamison and I were…we were just discussing a case."

"Everything okay with Mary?"

"Yes. Thanks for asking."

There was an awkward moment of silence. Could that be the only reason Sawyer had called? She felt the loss, the sense of disappointment spread through her body.

"I was wondering if you'd have time for a late dinner tonight. I know you're busy and all."

*Play a little hard to get.* Jamison's advice rang in her ears. Hell. It would be hard to pull that off when she threw herself at him later. "I'd love to."

"Great. I'll pick you up at seven."

*Come naked.* "I'll be ready." Liz hung up the phone.

When Mary walked by unexpectedly ten minutes later, Liz still stared at her blank computer screen, unable to get much past the fact that in just a few short hours, she'd have another opportunity to seduce the very serious Sawyer Montgomery.

"Hi, sweetie," she said when the young girl dropped into the chair in front of her desk. "How are you?"

"I'm starting to waddle."

"It always looked good on Donald and Daisy."

"I saw the doc this morning. He thinks the baby is already over seven pounds."

No wonder she beamed. "Good. Your due date is coming up fast."

"I know. I've been a real pain about this adoption thing.

I know you've been worried that time is going to run out. I've made up my mind."

"That's wonderful, Mary. I know it's been difficult. What do you want to do?"

"I'm giving her up for adoption."

"Her?"

"They did an ultrasound. The doc is ninety-nine percent sure the baby is a girl."

"And you're sure? About the adoption?" In her heart, she believed the decision was best for Mary and for the baby. Mary probably knew that, as well. Knowing it and acting upon it were two different things.

"Yes. I'm too young to raise a baby. I need to go back to school and get an education. I don't want to work in some stupid job my whole life. I'm going to go to college. Maybe that's selfish, but that's what I want."

"It's not selfish, Mary. You're young. You have hopes and dreams. College is one way to make those things a reality."

"You know what made me decide adoption was the right thing?"

"What?"

"I was thinking about all those things, and then I realized that I wanted my baby to have all the same things. But I'd never be able to give her that. That's what made me decide."

Mary wiped a tear off her face. Liz hoped she could be strong for both of them. "I'll contact our attorney. We'll get the paperwork done immediately."

"No."

"But, Mary, you just said—"

"You didn't let me finish. I'm giving her up for adoption under one condition. I want you to adopt her."

Liz felt the floor tip. "Mary. Sweetheart. I...I'm flattered. Really. But I can't possibly adopt your child."

"Why not? You already have your education and you

have a great job. You're home at night and on the weekends. You live in a safe apartment. You can give her everything she'll need."

She could. But that wasn't the point. "Mary," she said, not sure where to begin. "Any number of people have the means to provide for a child. That does not mean that they would be good parents."

"I know that. You couldn't grow up in my house and not realize that. But with you, it would be different. You would be such a great mom."

A mom. A single mother. A statistic. A concern.

But those were the black-and-white facts and figures. Liz knew better. While it wasn't a perfect solution, single mothers were quite capable of raising great, well-adjusted kids. But could she do it?

She hadn't thought about babies for herself. At least not since it had become abundantly clear that Ted never intended to marry her. While they'd been engaged, she often thought about the children she hoped to have. They'd talked about it. But when she'd finally stopped waiting for him, she'd stopped thinking about children, never considering pursuing motherhood on her own.

Why not? Why the heck not? Mary was right. She had a good job. Even if OCM wasn't around forever, she had the background and the credentials to land another job quickly. She had a nice savings account courtesy of her previous work. She was healthy and strong. She was—

"But the most important thing," Mary said, interrupting her thoughts, "is that you'll love her. And she'll love you."

Now Liz and Mary were both crying.

"Oh, Mary. Are you sure?"

"I'm sure. More sure about this than anything. Please say you'll do it."

It wasn't really much of a decision. How could she say no?

She loved Mary. By default, she loved the baby that Mary carried. She had a connection to this baby that would carry her through the difficult months to come. She could do this. She wanted to do this.

What would Sawyer think? Did it matter? She knew it did. They'd never even discussed children. There'd been no need to. She hoped he'd be happy for her, that he'd understand what a gift Mary had given her.

"I'd be honored, Mary. I will love her and care for her. When she grows up, I'll tell her about her biological mother and what a wonderful young woman she was."

Mary wrapped her arms around Liz. "Thank you. Now I know everything will be okay."

LIZ HAD A THREE-PAGE LIST by the time her hand cramped up, and she was forced to lay down her pen. So much to do and so little time. She had to get the spare bedroom decorated. She needed a crib, a car seat. Clothes. She needed to tell Jamison. He'd be worried about the appearance of things. After all, someone on the outside looking in would say it was unethical for a counselor to adopt the child of one of her clients. But that was the legal mumbo jumbo. On paper, it might look weird. In her heart, Liz knew it made perfect sense. She also knew that once Jamison got past his shock, he'd do everything he could to help her.

She didn't want to wait another minute to do it. She walked up the stairs to his office. He sat at his desk, calmly reviewing the budget numbers, not having any idea that she was about to upset his world. She almost felt sorry for him.

"I just talked to Mary Thorton. She's agreed to put her baby up for adoption."

"That's probably a good decision on her part."

"Yes. Here's the kicker, Jamison. She wants me to adopt the baby."

He pushed his chair back from the desk. "You told her no, I assume."

She shook her head, almost laughing when all color left his face. She felt so good about the decision that his doubts couldn't dispel her joy. "No. I said I would."

She gave Jamison a moment to recover before continuing, "I know it's highly irregular. I know others might question the decision. But you know me, Jamison. You know I wouldn't agree to this if it weren't the right thing for me and for the client. I can do this. I can adopt this baby and make a difference in the baby's life."

"But, Liz, you're a single woman. You know we always try to place the babies with two-parent families."

"I know. But we've made exceptions in the past. This is at the client's request. We always give special consideration to that."

He stared at her. Then he stood up, walked around his office twice, then sat down again. He didn't say a word. "You're sure?"

"Absolutely. I'm scared. I'm not going to try to lie about that. It's such a huge commitment. What if I'm no good at this?"

"You've been good at everything you've ever done."

Liz walked around the edge of the desk and placed her hand on Jamison's shoulder. "You know what drove me to OCM."

"Is that why you're doing this? Is this more of the same? More of having to make up for not being there?"

Liz didn't take offense. Jamison had always known her better than most. "No. Jenny's gone. I will forever miss her. I'm not doing this for her or because of her. I'm doing it for me. I pray that I'll be the kind of mother this sweet child deserves."

Jamison put his head in his hands. "We're going to need an ironclad release from Mary."

"She'll sign it," Liz said.

"I don't want her coming back in five years claiming that you coerced her into the decision. You don't want that."

She understood the legal issues. "You're right. That's why I'm here. I want you to handle the paperwork from here. I know you won't miss anything."

He looked up and let out a big sigh. "Okay. Let's call Howard. He's going to have to work his magic."

But Howard didn't answer. Jamison left a message on his machine. Liz got up from her chair, walked around the desk and kissed Jamison. "Thank you," she said. "Thank you for supporting me."

"What's your friend the cop going to say about this?"

She couldn't wait to tell Sawyer. Mary had barely been out the door, and Liz had been reaching for the telephone. She'd dialed the first five numbers before common sense prevailed. She couldn't just call him, chat about the weather for a couple of minutes and drop the bomb. *Hey, Sawyer. Great news. I'm adopting a baby.*

He might be worried that a baby would change their relationship. After all, she wouldn't be able to drop everything to go out to dinner. But babies did sleep. Maybe they could still work in sex and breakfast.

"I'm not sure what he'll say," she said. "I'll see him tonight."

## Chapter Fifteen

Sawyer rang her doorbell at seven minutes before seven. She looked out the peephole. He had on a blue sport coat, tan slacks and a white shirt. He looked good enough to eat.

She opened the door. "I've missed you," she said.

"Really?"

"Oh, yeah." She reached out, caught his striped tie in her hand and hauled him into the apartment. She released the tie, cradling his face with both hands. Then she kissed him. Hard.

She squirmed, pressed and arched, her hands racing across his back. She yanked at his coat. He helped, never taking his lips off hers. She pulled his shirt out of his pants, then grabbed for his belt buckle. Unzipping him, she boldly stuck her hand down his pants, wrapping her hand around him.

He bit her lip and pushed her against the wall. "Damn," he said.

"I want you inside me."

He grabbed her bottom, whipping his head up when he found nothing but skin under her dress. He stepped back and shucked his pants. Then he picked her up, braced her back against the wall, wrapped her legs around his waist, and in less than a minute, when she started to climax, he followed her over the edge.

Sawyer, his chest heaving, having come so hard he thought

he might pass out, gently unwrapped Liz's legs from his waist. He held her steady when she swayed. He rested his forehead against the wall, not certain if he'd ever be able to move.

The mantel clock chimed. Seven delicate rings.

Liz looked up and kissed his chin. "Thanks for coming early," she said.

He chuckled, knowing he didn't have the strength to laugh. He lifted his head and stepped back. His sport coat lay near the door. His pants and underwear a mere foot away. He'd taken her with his shirt and tie still on.

"You okay?" he asked.

"Wonderful."

"You look happy," he said.

"I am. I had a great day. How was yours?"

"Okay. I've got news about Mirandez," he said. He tucked his shirt in and zipped his pants. "Let's sit on the couch."

"Tell me," she said.

"We got Mirandez back to Chicago today. He's taken up residence at Cook County Jail. There's a hearing tomorrow. The judge will deny bail. That's a given."

"That's great."

"Yeah. There's something else. We had to turn over Mary's statement to his attorney. We put it off as long as we could."

"What should I tell Mary?"

"Tell her that we've arranged for her to go to a safe place. There's a hospital nearby. We've also arranged for help for a few weeks after the baby's born."

Mary wouldn't need help. "That won't be necessary."

"Are you sure? It's not a problem."

"Mary's giving the baby up for adoption. She wants to go to school. If there's no college nearby, you're going to have to pick a new place."

He looked a little shocked. "Yeah, actually, there's a great school about twenty minutes away. When did she decide all this?"

"Just today." This wasn't how she'd planned to tell him. He'd surprised her. It shouldn't matter. Maybe it just made everything easier. "Oh, Sawyer. The most wonderful thing has happened. Mary asked me to adopt her baby."

If he'd looked shocked before, now he looked absolutely stunned. She could see the color drain out of his face.

"What did you say?"

"Yes. I said yes. I'm adopting the baby. We think it's a girl."

"Are you crazy?" He stood up and paced around the room. "Have you lost your mind?"

She'd expected surprise. The anger hadn't even been on her radar screen. "Sawyer, what's wrong? You're acting weird."

"How could you do this? You have your career. You love your job. You told me so."

"I do love my job. But this gift, this totally unexpected, wonderful gift, has been given to me. I want the baby. I want to love her and watch her grow. I want to make a difference in her life. I want her to make a difference in mine."

"No."

He said the word as if it had two syllables, as if it had been torn from his soul.

"Sawyer, for God's sake, tell me what's wrong."

"I love you," he said. Where his voice had been loud before, it was now quiet. She could barely hear him. "I've loved you for weeks."

It should have made her dance with joy. But the anguish in his voice stopped her happiness cold.

"I wanted to give you time to get used to the idea. I didn't want to push. I wanted you to get used to me."

"Sawyer, I didn't know. I—"

"Now," he said, interrupting her, "everything has changed. I can't be with you."

Her chest hurt. She clenched her hands together.

"I don't understand," she said.

"I had a son," he said. "He died. In my arms. His tiny heart just couldn't do it."

A son. Why hadn't he ever told her?

"His mother?" she asked.

"Terrie was a young drug addict. I didn't know it when I got her pregnant. It was painfully clear by the time she'd had the baby. My son paid for her sins. He paid for my sins."

"Your sins?"

"I didn't protect him. I failed."

It started to make sense, in some horrible kind of way. "That's the girl who died? Your baby's mother died?"

"The drugs killed her, too. Just took a few years."

Oh, the pain he'd suffered. Liz wanted to reach out to him, to hold him, but she knew she had to hear it all.

"We never got married. I only saw her once after our son died. But I still didn't want her to die. It was just one more damn useless death."

His relentless passion for tracking Mirandez suddenly made a lot more sense. "Sawyer, I'm so sorry that happened to you. It must have been horrible."

"You have no idea."

She let that one pass. She hadn't lost a child. But she had lost a sister. She knew the emptiness, the absolute gray that had filled her world for months. She wouldn't try to compare her loss to his. To do so would trivialize both. "It was a long time ago, Sawyer. You have to move on."

"I moved on. I made a decision that I'd never father another child. I had a vasectomy ten years ago."

Well! How could she have fallen in love with a man she didn't really even know?

That wasn't exactly true. She knew Sawyer Montgomery. She knew what she needed to know. He was a good man, a loving man, capable of sacrificing his own safety to help a young, pregnant teen. She didn't want to lose him. "Sawyer, you have to let go. Not of the person, but of the anger, the absolute rage that you've lost someone."

The look he gave her was filled with contempt. "I'm not some jerk paying a hundred bucks an hour so that I can lie on your couch and you can try to heal me."

"Sawyer, that's not what this is. This is Liz and Sawyer, having a conversation. Nothing more. Nothing less."

"I'm not angry," he said. "Who the hell would I be angry at? A dead woman?"

She knew better than that. Even as a kid, Capable Sawyer would have wanted to handle everything. But he hadn't been able to handle this. He still hadn't forgiven himself. He tried to find peace. With every scumbag of a drug dealer he put away, he tried to buy peace. Only, peace wasn't for sale. It had to be delivered. That only happened when a person gave up the hate, the absolute despair of being left behind.

"You're asking me to choose between this baby and you," she said. "That's not fair. I shouldn't have to choose."

He looked at her, and a tear slipped out of his very brown eyes. He didn't bother to wipe it away. "No, you shouldn't," he said. "I can't let another child into my life. I won't risk it."

Liz's heart, which had started to crumble away at the edges, suddenly broke right down the middle. The pain, as real as if the strong muscle really could just crack, sliced through her body.

With trembling legs, she walked over to the door and opened it. Not able to look at him again, she stared at the floor. "I'm sorry about your son. If I had known, I'd have done this differently."

"You're saying you wouldn't adopt the child?"

"No, I'm not saying that. But I wouldn't have just blurted it out. You should have told me. Everything now seems like such a lie."

He slammed his hand against the wall. "I never lied to you."

"You let me think you were in love with your dead girl-friend. I had no idea that there had even been a child. You lied by omission. For God's sake, Sawyer. You let me worry about an unplanned pregnancy."

He didn't respond. She didn't really expect him to. She suddenly felt very old, as if her bones might splinter. She forced herself to straighten up, to lift her head. "I don't want to see you again," she said. "Jamison can be your contact. Give him the details about the arrangements for Mary."

LIZ HAD BEEN IN BED for just a few minutes when the tele-phone rang. "Hello," she answered.

"Liz, it's Mary. My water just broke."

Liz sat up in bed, fear and excitement making her heart race. "Have you been in labor long? How far apart are your contractions?"

"Hey, you sound strange. What's wrong?"

Liz covered the phone and cleared her throat. She'd spent the better part of the past hour crying. Her eyes burned, she could barely swallow and her head felt as if she'd been kicked. "I've got a touch of a cold. Nothing to worry about. Now, what about the contractions?"

"I'm not having contractions. I don't think I'm even in labor."

"You're sure? No pain of any kind?"

"My back has ached all day," Mary said.

While Liz was no expert on childbirth, she had heard about back labor. She wanted Mary at a hospital. Now. "Honey, do you think you can take a cab to the hospital?"

"Yeah."

"Perfect. I'll meet you there. We should arrive about the same time. Just hang on. And breathe. Don't forget to breathe."

She'd arranged just that morning for her car to be picked up and the dents repaired. She grabbed the phone book out of the drawer, dialed the number for the cab company and waited impatiently while it rang three times. They said ten minutes and she was ready in eight. The ride to the hospital seemed to take forever. Yet, still, she beat Mary's cab by ten minutes. When it finally pulled up, she yanked open the back door. She helped Mary out and threw a twenty at the driver.

"How are you?" she asked, hoping she didn't sound as scared as she was.

"I don't want to have a baby," Mary said. "I'm not doing this."

Liz wrapped her arms around the girl, holding her close. "Don't worry. It'll be over in no time."

No time turned out to be twelve hours later. Twelve long, ugly hours filled with swearing, yelling, moaning, groaning and crying. But when Liz placed the beautiful baby girl in Mary's arms, the look on the girl's face told her that it had all been worth it.

"She's so pretty," Mary said, stroking the baby's head and face. "Isn't her mouth just perfect?"

Liz nodded. The baby was a healthy seven pounds and two ounces and just eighteen inches long. Almost plump. The doctor had delivered her and said, "Look at those cheeks." He hadn't been talking about her face.

"She's gorgeous," Liz said.

Mary stared at the baby. "I love her," she said, her voice filled with awe. "I just love her so much."

How could anyone not love something so perfect, so absolutely perfect in every way? Liz swallowed, almost afraid to ask the next question. She'd known she was taking a chance by letting Mary hold the baby. But Mary had been explicit. She wanted to see her child.

"Having second thoughts about giving her up for adoption?" Liz asked, wondering if she could slip back into the role of counselor after having embraced the role of mother.

"I'm not giving her up."

Liz nodded, afraid to speak.

"I'm giving her to you. That's different. I'm giving her to someone that I know will care for her and love her and give her all the things that I can't give her."

Liz didn't think her legs would continue to hold her. She sank down onto the edge of the bed. "Are you sure, Mary? Are you absolutely sure?"

"Yes. I've screwed up most of my life. I'm not screwing this up. She's my daughter. That will never change. But she's your daughter, too. She's going to call you Mom. And you're going to take her to her first day of kindergarten and make her Halloween costumes and make sure she has braces and gets into a good college. I know you'll do that. If you're half as good to her as you've been to me, she'll be a very happy girl."

Liz couldn't have stopped the tears if she'd tried. But she didn't. She let them fall, in celebration of mothers and daughters, in thanks of second chances, in hopes that Mary would someday have another daughter to love. In a different time, in a different place.

Mary held the baby out to Liz. "Here, take your daughter. She needs to start getting used to you. What are you going to name her?"

"I don't know. I hadn't thought about it."

"Would you call her Catherine? That was my mother's name."

Liz swallowed hard. "Catherine is a beautiful name. She fits it perfectly."

LIZ HELD CATHERINE for two hours before finally returning her to the nursery. She left the hospital, choosing to walk instead of catching a cab. She needed the fresh air. It had been a long stretch in a stuffy hospital.

She also needed to call Jamison. He had to get Mary's signature on the adoption agreement and get Catherine released to a temporary foster home for a couple of days. Liz hated that part. She wanted to bring her daughter home right away. But she knew the rules. She wasn't going to do anything that would jeopardize the legal standing of the adoption.

By the time Liz could pick up Catherine, she assumed Mary would be well on her way to her new home. Mary had accepted the news that she would be relocated under the witness-protection program with cautious optimism. Liz knew the young girl was scared but that she also welcomed the chance to have a new life.

At one point in the discussion, Mary had joked about calling Sawyer to thank him. Liz hadn't been able to even smile. The pain of losing Sawyer tasted too fresh, too bitter.

She would go on. She had Catherine. She had her work. Assuming Jamison would let her bring Catherine with her. That was just one more thing to talk to him about. She pulled her cell phone out of her purse. She'd called him shortly after she and Mary had arrived at the hospital last night. But then things had gotten a little hectic.

Jamison answered on the first ring. "Yes," he said.

"Jamison, it's Liz. It's over. She had a little girl. She's a beauty."

"Mom and baby okay?"

"Yes. Pretty tough delivery but Mary did great."

"Did she hold the baby?"

"Yes. And then she handed her to me and said that I better get to know my daughter."

For once, Jamison seemed speechless.

"Have you heard from Detective Montgomery?" Liz asked.

"Yes. He called late last night. I told him Mary was in labor. He said he would have some guards posted outside of Mary's room. Did you see them?"

She had. She'd appreciated them, but it had been just one more painful reminder of the man she'd loved and lost. He took care of things. He made things happen. He made it tough on the bad guys. "Yes, I did."

"I'm supposed to call him once I talk to you. They want to move Mary as soon as possible. He was going to have somebody talk to the doctor."

She knew it was for the best, but it still hurt to know that she would soon lose Mary from her life. "She can't be moved until she signs the adoption agreement. Or, at the very least, she needs to be moved somewhere we can get to her. You need to call and tell him that."

"Why can't you call him?"

She didn't bother to answer.

"What's going on here?" Jamison asked.

She didn't want to talk about it. Not yet. She'd managed not to think about Sawyer the entire time Mary had been in labor. She couldn't let her mind go there yet. She wasn't ready. "Jamison, I know I'm not making much sense. But you need to trust me."

"I don't understand."

"I'm not going to be seeing Sawyer again. I want something that he won't let himself have."

"It's still not all that clear," Jamison said.

"I don't understand it. Why should you?"

"You okay?"

Trust Jamison to get down to the nitty-gritty. "Yes. I'm fine. And next week, I'll be better. And in a year or two, I might even be good."

"Anything I can do?"

"Yes. Get that paperwork to Mary. I want to bring my daughter home."

Liz put her cell phone away. She walked another two blocks to the grocery store. There she filled her cart with bottles, formula, diapers and lotion. The next stop was a department store. She got some blankets, T-shirts and one-piece sleepers. She knew she'd need a hundred more things but she could always ask Carmen or Jamison to help her out.

Funny. When Mary had first asked her to adopt the baby, Liz had thought Sawyer would be around to help. Had looked forward to sharing the baby with him. That wouldn't happen. And she needed to stop hoping, stop praying that it might change. He was gone. She better start getting used to it.

When she got home, she dropped her purchases on the kitchen counter and went back to her bedroom, taking her clothes off on the way, leaving just her bra and panties on. She lay back on the bed, closed her eyes and assumed sleep would come. After all, she'd been up for thirty-some hours. But sleep, being a slippery fellow, danced just out of her grasp. She tossed and turned, her body too keyed up to get any real rest. After an hour, she got up.

She made herself a cup of tea and a grilled-cheese sandwich. She checked her voice mail. No calls. Not able to be patient, she dialed Jamison's number.

"Yes," he said.

"Have you been to see Mary? Did she sign?"

"You should be sleeping, Liz."

"I know. Well?"

"It's the strangest thing. I can't get in touch with Howard. He's not answering his cell phone. I've left four messages on his pager, and his assistant doesn't know where he is."

Howard Fraypish was never unreachable. He carried a backup cell just in case his primary one went dead. "Are you sure you have the right number?" She rattled it off.

"I know the number. I've left messages. I can't do anything until I get the paperwork from him."

If Mary hadn't gone into labor a week early, Liz would have had all the loose ends tied up. Now she needed Howard. "I'll go over to his office."

"He's not there."

"Maybe his assistant can find the documents on his PC. She'll print them off for me. I've known her for years."

On her way out of the apartment, she stopped to check her mailbox in the odd event that Howard had mailed the information to her. She opened the slot and pulled out an assortment of bills, a magazine and…a plain white envelope with her name scratched across it.

She slid her thumb under the flap and pulled out the single sheet.

Stay away from Mary Thorton and her baby. Otherwise, they die. You don't want that on your conscience.

Liz slammed her mailbox shut. Damn it. It was supposed to be over. Mirandez was in jail. She waited for the fear to hit her, but all she could feel was bone-deep anger. Somebody had threatened Catherine. Her child.

She would not let them win.

She grabbed both the envelope and the sheet of paper by the edges and slid them into her purse. Once she'd seen Howard, she would take the letter to the police.

"I'm sorry, Liz. Howard didn't leave any paperwork for either you or Jamison."

She was not in the mood to be put off. "Can't you just get it off his computer?"

The woman looked a little shocked. "I don't know his password," she said. "Even if I did, I'm not sure that would be appropriate."

"Look, Helen. What's inappropriate is for Howard to have left his office without providing us with the necessary paperwork to complete this adoption. Now he won't return any calls. I want to know what's going on. This is so unlike him."

Now the woman looked really nervous. "I...I'm not sure what's going on," she confessed. "Howard has been acting so strange. Real nervous. Almost jumpy. Have you seen him lately?"

"Yes." She'd seen him at the hospital when Melissa Stroud had her baby. "He seemed a little scatterbrained but nothing unusual for Howard."

"Twice in the past week, I've caught him sleeping at his desk in the middle of the afternoon. When I arrive in the mornings, I can tell he's been working all night."

It didn't sound good, but then again, she had her own sleep issues. "Maybe he's just working too hard. Does he have new clients?"

The woman shook her head. "No, just the opposite. Business is off. If it wasn't for OCM and a couple other agencies that he works with, I'm not sure I'd have a desk to sit at. Last week I wanted to order a new fax machine and he told me to hold off—that cash was a little tight this month."

Liz did not have time to worry about Howard. She had plenty of her own worries. She stood up and slung the strap of her purse over her shoulder. "If you talk to him, tell him it's imperative that he call Jamison. We need the paperwork, and we need it now. If I don't have it within twelve hours,

I'm going to recommend to Jamison that OCM find a new attorney."

Liz left Howard's office and tried to grab a cab to take her to the police department. Two passed her by without even slowing down. In her hurry to leave the apartment, she'd forgotten her cell phone. She changed her path and headed back toward her apartment. Once there, she could call for a cab.

She was four blocks from home when three men jumped out of the bushes. All three wore dark coats and blue jeans, and each had a ski mask over his face.

Liz looked around for help, but the residential street was empty. "What do you want?" she asked, forcing words around her fear.

"Shut up," one man said. Then he put his hand on her shoulder and pushed her hard. Liz stumbled back and stuck both arms out, breaking her fall. Sharp rocks cut into the palms of her hand. She scrambled to her feet, unwilling to let them tower over her.

Another man grabbed for her purse, yanking it so hard that the shoulder strap broke. Liz didn't try to fight him for it. The first man stepped forward again. Liz braced herself for another push. She didn't expect the fist to her jaw, sending rockets of pain through her whole face.

She tasted blood.

"You stay away from Mary Thorton and her baby," the third man said. "If you don't, you'll be sorry. This is just a little sample. Just because Dantel's in jail doesn't mean he's not still in charge." Then he hit her in the stomach. She doubled over. When she managed to catch her breath and straighten up, they were gone.

It had all happened in less than a minute. She'd been attacked in broad daylight. She took stock of her injuries. She gently moved her jaw back and forth, very grateful when everything seemed to work. Blood oozed from several small cuts on the palms of her hands. She bent down to pick up her purse, and pain shot through her midsection. Damn. She probably had a broken rib or two. She sank to her knees and managed to grab the strap. Awkwardly, she got to her feet and half walked, half ran the rest of the way to her apartment.

Once inside, she got to the sink and spit out the blood in her mouth. She walked over to the telephone, careful not to look in the mirror on the way, and dialed 911.

# Chapter Sixteen

Two officers and an ambulance responded. The police questioned her briefly. She gave them the best description she could of the men and told them what they'd said about Dantel Mirandez. She handed over the letter and envelope. Then the ambulance transported her to the hospital, the same one she'd left just hours earlier literally walking on air. Now she lay flat on her back, wheeled in, presented to the nurse on duty like a stuffed turkey on Thanksgiving Day.

The doctor put six stitches in the inside of her cheek, where her teeth had cut into the tender flesh. He also cleaned out the rocks in her hands and wrapped them up in white gauze. Then someone else took films of her ribs and substantiated that one was cracked. The doctor didn't even bother to wrap it, just told her to move carefully for a couple days.

She'd just snapped her jeans when Sawyer burst into the exam room. When he saw her, he stopped so suddenly that his body almost pitched forward over his feet.

He stared at her. First at her swollen jaw, then at her wrapped hands. When he finally spoke, his voice seemed rusty, as if he hadn't used it for a while.

"Are you okay?" The minute he said it, he knew it was an insane question. One look at her told him she wasn't okay.

"How did you know I was here?" she asked.

"The responding officers ran Mirandez's name through

the database. I came up as the arresting officer. So, they called me."

It sounded so simple. It didn't give any clue to the absolute terror he'd felt when they'd told him about her injuries. "He'll pay for this," Sawyer told her. "I promise you. He will pay for this."

She didn't say anything. Just stood there, holding her blouse together with one hand. He could see the pale blue silk of her bra against her soft skin. So beautiful. So fragile.

It was his fault this had happened. He never should have let Lieutenant Fischer talk him into taking her to Wisconsin in the first place. Mirandez wouldn't have any reason to be going after her now.

"I'm sorry," he said. "I'm sorry that bastard hurt you. I'm sorry I let him."

She looked at him as if he'd lost his mind.

He tried again. "I expected him to go after Mary. I never thought you'd be the target. That was stupid of me. Now you're paying the price."

She dismissed his concerns with a wave of her free hand. "How could you have known? He's been told the baby isn't his. Why would he care about warning me away from Mary or the baby? Did they tell you about the letter?"

"I swung by the station and took a look at it. He spelled your name right this time," Sawyer said, feeling the disgust well up in the back of his throat.

"I guess I didn't notice," she said.

"What exactly did the men say to you?" Sawyer asked. "Word for word, if you can remember."

"They told me to stay away from Mary and the baby. Then they said that just because Dantel was behind bars it didn't mean he wasn't still in charge."

Sawyer rubbed his forehead. He had a hell of a headache. It didn't make sense. None of it. Not that he questioned that

Mirandez had been able to communicate with his gang. That happened all the time. Prison bars didn't prove to be a very strong barrier. Sometimes it was a phone conversation in code. Other times, a dirty guard willing to carry messages back and forth for a price.

Perhaps the order had come down before Mirandez learned that the baby wasn't his. Whatever the reason, Sawyer would find out. "Is it okay for you to leave?" he asked.

She nodded. "Yes."

"I'll take you home."

"No." The word exploded from her. He hadn't expected less.

"Liz, be reasonable. You're hurt. You can't walk home. Just let me drive you." He wanted to make sure she got safely inside her apartment. It was the least he could do.

"No," she repeated. "I'm not ready to leave. I want to see Mary as long as I'm here."

"I'll wait," he said.

"That's not necessary," she said.

She looked as if she'd rather be anywhere but with him. He couldn't blame her. "We're moving Mary tomorrow," he said. "Guards will remain outside her door until then. We're placing a plainclothes cop in the nursery just in case he'd go for...the baby."

"Her name is Catherine."

Catherine. He didn't want to know that. Didn't want to know anything about the baby. But Liz deserved to know that her baby would be safe. "Your boss told me that the baby goes to a temporary foster home for a couple days. The detective can go with her just in case."

She chuckled, a dry, humorless laugh. "The foster parents should love that."

"It's not great, I agree. But it beats the alternative."

"What happens when I bring her home? Does the detective stay until she's in college?"

He could hear the sarcasm. "I don't think that will be necessary. But maybe for a couple of weeks. We're having the doctor certify that Mary was at or near a full-term pregnancy. We'll provide that to Mirandez's attorney. Just in case, we're asking permission from the court to run a DNA match. We need to get a blood draw from Mirandez. That will prove conclusively that he's not the father. But it will take several weeks before those results are available."

"Capable Sawyer."

"What?"

"Never mind. It was stupid. I'm just tired. I need to see Mary. You need to leave." She buttoned her shirt. He looked away, not wanting to watch her hands, not wanting to think about how his own hands had unbuttoned her shirt, how he had literally shook with wanting her.

Because perhaps, in a lifetime or two, he might forget.

He heard her groan. She had her sweater half-on with one sleeve hanging free. The arm that should have filled it was wrapped around her waist. She was even paler than before. "What's wrong?"

"Cracked rib."

He hadn't thought he could hate Mirandez any more than he already did. "Any other injuries that I can't see?" he asked. He knew she hadn't been raped. When the officers had contacted him, he'd asked that. Knowing that if she had, he'd have killed the men responsible. He would have laid down his badge and gone after them and ripped their hearts out.

She shook her head. "No. All in all, I think I got lucky."

Lucky. As absurd as it sounded, she was right. With no witnesses to stop them, it would have been easy for Mirandez's men to slit her throat or put a bullet through her temple. But they hadn't. They'd roughed her up and scared her, but they'd left her standing.

He took a step forward, then another, stopping just a foot away from her. Gently, he took her arm and pushed it through the sweater sleeve. With unsteady hands, he pulled both sides together, fastening the top button. Then the second one. The third.

Liz didn't breathe. Couldn't. Sawyer had his head bent, concentrating as he worked the buttons into the small holes, his strong fingers being so careful, so gentle. She thought her legs might not hold her. The man was helping her, dressing her like an adult would a child, and it was the most erotic thing that had ever happened to her.

When he finished with the last button, he lifted his head, meeting her eyes. He leaned forward, and ever so softly, he brushed his lips across her sore and swollen jaw. Then he reached for her bandaged hands, raised each one to his lips and gently kissed the tips of her fingers.

Then he gathered her small hands in his much larger ones, brought them to his chest and bent his head forward so that his forehead rested on hers. She could feel the beat of his heart pulsing through her body, sending crazy, wild, zigzag waves through her. His breath was hot, his skin cool, his body strong. She felt safe and protected. Yet weak and wanting for more.

"I love you," he said, his voice just a whisper in her ear. "I'm so sorry you got hurt."

She took in a deep breath, wanting to always remember the scent of Sawyer. She focused on his hands, which were still wrapped around hers. She wanted to remember the feel of his skin, the lines of his bones, the strength of his muscles. It wouldn't be enough. But it would be all she had.

"Sawyer, you need to go." She said it softly, all the malice gone. He was a good man. He'd suffered a great loss. She didn't want to drag out the goodbyes, making either one of them suffer more.

He nodded and pulled his hands away. He looked her straight in the eye. He slowly raised his right hand, reaching toward her face. She caught his fingers with her own and gently pushed his hand back to his side. Then she deliberately and carefully reached up and on her own, all on her own, tucked the wayward strand of hair behind her ear.

He gave her a sad half smile. Without another word, he left the room.

THE NEXT MORNING, Sawyer waited impatiently while they brought Mirandez up to see him. The door opened, and his slimy attorney came in first, carrying a briefcase almost bursting at the seams. Mirandez shuffled in next, his hands cuffed in front of him.

Sawyer hadn't wanted to come. He didn't want to even look at the murdering bastard. But he'd come up empty-handed in his search for the men who had terrorized Liz. Even the guys on the inside couldn't shake loose any information.

"This is highly irregular, Detective," the attorney said, setting his briefcase down on the table with a thud. "What is it that's so important that you had to talk to my client at the crack of dawn? It's barely seven o'clock."

He didn't care whose butt he'd had to drag out of bed. He'd been up all night. But still he had nothing. "Your client arranged to have Liz Mayfield beaten and threatened."

"That's impossible," the attorney said, disregarding Sawyer's statement.

Sawyer didn't bother to respond. He'd been studying Mirandez. For the briefest second, the man had looked surprised, then he'd completely closed down, pulling his usual sneer back in place.

"Are you charging him?"

"I want to ask him some questions."

"Under the circumstances, I will advise my client not to answer."

Mirandez sat up straighter in his chair. "Shut up, Bill. You talk too damn much."

The attorney's face turned red. Sawyer almost felt sorry for him until he remembered that the guy made his living defending killers. He deserved to be treated like dirt.

Mirandez rocked back in his chair. "Do you lie awake at night thinking these things, Cop?"

Mirandez was half-right. Since he'd let Liz slip out of his life, Sawyer had spent most of his nights staring at the ceiling, afraid to close his eyes, afraid to give in to the temptation to remember what it felt like to be wrapped in her arms. Last night, after walking away from her yet again, he'd worked himself to death, poring over reports, talking to informants, hoping he could forget the look in her eyes when she'd told him goodbye.

"You need to hire better help," Sawyer said. "Your guys ID'd you. They said you sent them. We've got both letters. You're not going to get away with this."

"You bore me." Mirandez put both hands on the table and twirled his thumbs. "What do you think I am? Stupid?"

"I think you're the scum of the earth."

Mirandez laughed. "Yes, well, I think you're pretty much an SOB yourself."

"Mr. Mirandez," the attorney began before a sharp look from his client had him shutting his mouth.

Mr. Mirandez? How freaking much was Mirandez paying the guy to get him to suck up that way? There wasn't enough money in the world. *Mr. Mirandez?* It made Sawyer sick. Nobody in his right mind would give Mirandez that kind of respect.

As suddenly as that, Sawyer figured it out. Mirandez. Not Mr. Mirandez, not Dantel Mirandez. He only went by Mirandez. Mary called him Dantel. Nobody else did. Nobody in his gang would. They probably didn't even know his first name.

"The baby isn't even mine. I don't care what happens to it."

Whoever had sent the men hadn't known that the baby wasn't Mirandez's. The men had warned Liz to stay away from Dantel's baby. Someone smart enough to throw the blame on Mirandez had hurt Liz. Why? Who? Would they try again?

Sawyer stood and grabbed his coat.

"Hey, what's your hurry?" Mirandez looked around the room. "While it's not Vegas, I thought we might play some cards. I'll stake you a couple hundred. I know you cops don't make much of a living."

"At least we make it honestly," Sawyer said and left before he followed through on his urge to slam Mirandez up against the wall.

He walked to his car, dialing Liz's number on his cell. The phone rang four times then the voice mail kicked on. He didn't want to leave a message. Wasn't sure what he even had to tell her. Just knew he needed to talk to her, needed to hear her voice. Needed to know that she was okay. He dialed OCM's main number next. Jamison answered on the second ring.

"Yes."

"Jamison, it's Sawyer Montgomery. I'm trying to get in touch with Liz. Is she there by any chance?"

"No. I haven't heard from her. She's supposed to be here at noon. We're meeting with Howard Fraypish. I talked to her early this morning. She had some errands to run and then she planned to stop by. I'll let her know to call you."

"Do that."

He redialed Liz's number. This time, when the voice mail kicked on, he left a brief message. "Liz, it's Sawyer. I don't think it was Mirandez's guys who attacked you. So, be careful, okay? Please call me. I know you probably don't want to talk to me. But just let me know you're okay. That's all you have to do. Just let me know."

He hung up before he started to beg. He couldn't shake the feeling that Liz was in danger. Not knowing what else to do, he drove. He went to Liz's apartment and pounded on the door. He dialed her number again and again. When her voice mail kicked on the last time, he said, "Liz, damn you, where are you? Call me."

He called Mary's room at the hospital. She hadn't seen her. He got the number of Randi's apartment and called there just in case. No luck. He called Robert and told him what was going on.

He was going to be too late. Something horrible had happened to Liz, and he was going to lose her. She'd never know how much he loved her. He hadn't been able to tell her. He'd chosen to let her believe that it wasn't enough.

*Life is about choices.* That was what she'd told him. Liz had chosen to live. She'd survived her sister's death, she'd learned to let go, to forgive herself for not being there. She'd chosen to make a difference in the lives of countless young women, allowing them to fully understand and appreciate that no matter how desperate the situation, they always had a choice.

They could lie or tell the truth. Give or take. Laugh or cry. Love or be empty forever.

Sawyer wiped the tears from his eyes as he drove down the familiar street. Without thinking, he went to the one place that gave him peace. He found his regular spot and parked the car. It had started to rain. It didn't matter. The cold, wet day couldn't touch him. He opened the gate of the small cemetery nestled between a church and a school. He took the path to the left. Then he knelt next to his son's grave and placed a hand on the shiny marker.

When he'd left Baton Rouge, his son had come with him. It had been the only choice.

The rain fell harder, hitting his head, his face, mixing with the tears that ran freely down his cheeks. He couldn't hear a thing besides the beating of his own heart.

Choices. He didn't want to give up his last chance to make the right one.

So, he bent his head, all the way to the ground, and he kissed the wet, cold earth that sheltered his child. He didn't kiss him goodbye. Never that. His son would always have a special place in his heart. But his heart needed to be bigger now. It needed to hold Liz and Catherine.

He'd been a coward. He knew now that he'd rather have one minute, one day, one week with Liz than a lifetime of being alone and afraid.

He knew he couldn't keep Liz or Catherine safe from all harm. He couldn't wrap them up in cotton and hide them from the danger that lurked in dark corners. They might get hurt. They might get sick. But he wanted to be there every step of the way, holding them, supporting them, making sure they knew they were loved more than life itself.

WHEN HE GOT BACK to the car, he tried Liz's apartment again. Still no answer. He checked his machine at work. No messages. Damn it.

He checked the time. Ten minutes after ten. Jamison had said they had a meeting with Fraypish at noon. Not knowing what else to do, Sawyer tried Jamison again.

"Yes," Jamison answered.

"It's Sawyer Montgomery. Any word from Liz?"

"No. I've tried a couple times. I swear this meeting is doomed. I can't reach Howard, either."

Fraypish. Liz had gone to see him and then been attacked. "Jamison, how well do you know Howard Fraypish?"

"We're like brothers. Why?"

"I don't know. It's just that there's something about him that nags at me."

"He's odd, but if you're thinking that he would harm Liz, that just wouldn't happen. When Liz got that first death threat from Dantel, Howard was just outraged."

Sawyer remembered Liz standing outside the hotel, whispering, *He doesn't know about the letter. Please don't tell him.*

"How did he know about the letter, Jamison?"

"I don't know. I might have mentioned it, I suppose."

A slow burn started in Sawyer's stomach. Mirandez's goons hadn't written the second letter. No, it had been somebody who knew about the first letter but hadn't actually seen it. Somebody who hadn't realized that Mayfield had been spelled wrong or that the grammar had been rough. Somebody who knew how to spell *conscience* and what it meant. Somebody who knew Mirandez as Dantel. That was what Mary called him. Sometimes Liz, too, especially after she'd been talking with Mary. Jamison had just referred to him as Dantel. That was likely the name he'd used when he'd been chatting with his buddy.

Sawyer turned a sharp left. "Jamison, what's Fraypish's address?"

The man hesitated, then rattled it off.

Sawyer hung up, called for backup and started praying. He couldn't lose her now. Not when he'd just found himself.

When he got there, he parked his car in front of the three-story brownstone. He took the steps two at a time. He had his fist just inches away from the door, ready to knock, when he heard a crash inside the house. He put his ear to the door and pulled his gun out of his holster. He could hear Liz and then another voice. An angry voice. A man's voice.

She was alive. He stepped away from the door, pulled out his cell phone and called for backup. He debated all of two seconds before he tried the handle. Locked. He heard a car pull up and realized that Jamison had also come.

He held up a finger warning the man to be quiet. "Do you have a key?"

"Yes. I feed his cats when he's not home." Jamison pulled out a ring and pointed at a gold key.

Sawyer inserted it quietly and opened the door just inches. He could hear their voices more clearly. Fraypish was yelling.

"You stupid woman. I am not going to let you ruin everything."

"Howard, you're never going to get away with it."

"I've been getting away with it for months. Your boss, Jamison, my good buddy, always was a trusting soul. And a fool."

"Why, Howard? At least tell me why you had to sell the babies."

"I'm not lucky at cards. At craps, either."

"How could you?"

Sawyer could hear the disgust in Liz's voice. Silently, he made his way down the hall.

"Easy. You'd be amazed at how desperate some people are to have a baby. Especially healthy, white infants like your little Catherine. They'll borrow from friends and family, mortgage their house. Whatever it takes. They'll drop a hundred thousand without blinking an eye."

"You make me sick," Liz said.

"You don't understand, Liz. I tried to convince you to stay away from that baby. When that didn't work, I hired a few guys to make my point. But still, you won't stop. I have to stop you."

"Howard, please, don't do this. We'll talk to Jamison. We'll get you help."

"It's too late. I borrowed money from the wrong people. If I don't make regular payments, they'll hurt me. Bad. They're due a check this week. I don't have any other babies in the pipeline. I need yours."

"You'll never get away with it. Jamison will figure it out."

"No, he won't. When you don't show up for the noon meeting, Jamison and I'll come looking for you. We'll find the body, I'll console Jamison, and your little Catherine will be on the market by dinnertime."

With that, Sawyer came around the corner. With one sharp downward thrust on Fraypish's arm, he knocked the gun out of his hand. Then he tackled the man, sending his fist into the guy's jaw. That was for the bruised jaw. He hit him again. That was for the cracked rib. He had his arm pulled back, ready to swing again, when two sets of hands pulled him off Fraypish.

"That's enough, Detective. We'll take it from here."

Sawyer shook his head to clear it. Two officers stood on each side of him. He took a step back. Liz sat on the bed, her arms wrapped around her middle. Tears ran down her face.

He pulled her into his arms.

"Thank you for getting here in time," she whispered. "I feel so stupid. I had no idea."

He held her. "Me, neither, honey. I focused on Mirandez, and I missed Fraypish."

"It's not your fault," she assured him.

Maybe not but he couldn't even think about what might have happened if he'd arrived five minutes later. He pulled back, just far enough that he could see her eyes. "I love you," he said, not willing to go another second without her knowing exactly how he felt. "I've been a stupid fool. I don't want to lose you. Tell me I haven't lost you. Tell me I'm not too late."

"What about your son?"

He brushed a tear off her cheek. "I loved him before he was born. Once I'd held him, he was the moon and stars and everything that was perfect. And when you love that much and you can't hold on to it, it hurts. It rips you apart. I didn't ever want to hurt like that again."

She kissed him, a whisper of lips against his cheek. "I never meant to hurt you."

"You were right. Life is about choices. When you love someone, there's a risk. You can choose to avoid risks, to never take the big leap off the cliff into the water, but then you never know the absolute joy of coming to the surface, the stunning glory of the bright sunshine in your eyes. I don't want to stand at the top alone."

"What are you saying?"

"Liz, I'm ready to jump. You have my heart. Take my hand. And together, with Catherine, we'll build a family. I'll take care of you, I promise. I love you. Please say you'll try."

She kissed him on the lips, and he allowed himself to hope. "You are the kindest, most loving and most…capable man I've ever met. I know you'll take care of me. I want a chance to take care of you." She reached out and took his hand. "And I want us to take care of our daughter together."

\* \* \* \* \*

# REQUEST YOUR FREE BOOKS!
## 2 FREE NOVELS PLUS 2 FREE GIFTS!

**HARLEQUIN®**

# INTRIGUE®

## BREATHTAKING ROMANTIC SUSPENSE

SPECIAL EXCERPT FROM

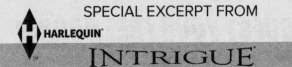

**HARLEQUIN**

# INTRIGUE

*When Jacie Kosart's twin sister needs rescuing from a dangerous drug cartel, she turns to tortured former FBI agent Zachary Adams. But can Zach put aside his own demons to help a beautiful damsel in distress?*

Read on for a sneak peek of

# TAKING AIM
*by*

## Elle James

Zach staggered back. The force with which the woman hit him knocked him back several steps before he could get his balance. He wrapped his arm around her automatically, steadying her as her knees buckled and she slipped toward the floor.

"Please, help me," she sobbed.

"What's wrong?" He scooped her into his arms and carried her through the open French doors into his bedroom and laid her on the bed.

Boots clattered on the wooden slats of the porch, and more came running down the hallway. Two of Hank's security guards burst into Zach's room through the French doors at the same time Hank entered from the hallway.

The security guards stood with guns drawn, their black-clad bodies looking more like ninjas than billionaire bodyguards.

"It's okay, I have everything under control," Zach said. Though he doubted seriously he had anything under control. He had no idea who this woman was or what she'd meant by *help me*.

HIEXP0813

Hank burst through the bedroom door, his face drawn in tense lines. "What's going on? I heard the sound of an engine outside and shouting coming from this side of the house." He glanced at Zach's bed and the woman stirring against the comforter. "What do we have here?"

She pushed to a sitting position and blinked up at Zach. "Where am I?"

"You're on the Raging Bull Ranch."

"Oh, dear God." She pushed to the edge of the bed and tried to stand. "I have to get back. They have her. Oh, sweet Jesus, they have Tracie."

Zach slipped an arm around her waist and pulled her to him to keep her from falling flat on her face again. "Where do you have to get back to? And who's Tracie?"

"Tracie's my twin. We were leading a hunting party on the Big Elk. They shot, she fell, now they have her." The woman grabbed Zach's shirt with both fists. "You have to help her."

"You're not making sense. Slow down, take a deep breath and start over."

"We don't have time!" The woman pushed away from Zach and raced for the French doors. "We have to get back before they kill her." She stumbled over a throw rug and hit the hardwood floor on her knees. "I shouldn't have left her." She buried her face in her hands and sobbed.

Zach stared at the woman, a flash of memory anchoring his feet to the floor.

*Don't miss the second book in the*
COVERT COWBOYS, INC. *series, TAKING AIM by Elle James.*

*Available July 23, only from Harlequin Intrigue.*

# SADDLE UP AND READ 'EM!

**This summer, get your fix of Western reads and pick up a cowboy from the SUSPENSE category in July!**

OUTLAW LAWMAN by Delores Fossen,
The Marshals of Maverick County
Harlequin Intrigue

TRIGGERED by Elle James,
Covert Cowboys, Inc.
Harlequin Intrigue

*Look for these great Western reads AND MORE,
available wherever books are sold or visit*
**www.Harlequin.com/Westerns**